A COMPLETELY ACCURATE PORTRAYAL
OF THE FUTURE

Read the continuing adventures at
www.starslip.com

First printing. Fourth in the book series. Contains material originally published at www.starslip.com.

ISBN 978-0-9797222-9-5

Published by Nightlight Press
www.nightlightpress.com

Printed in Canada

To starting over

A Completely Accurate Portrayal of the Future

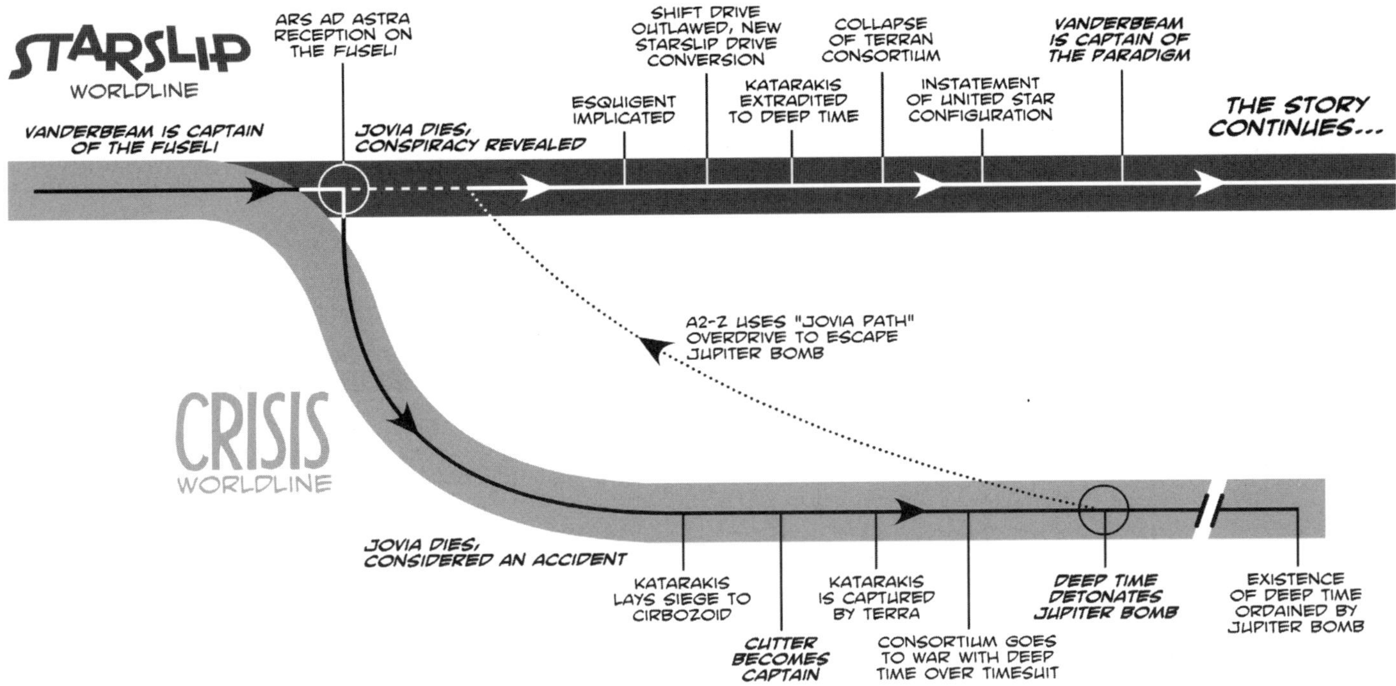

It is a new era.

In the 35th Century use of cheap, powerful Shift Drive technology created a Crisis which threatened both the present and future, known space finds itself at a crossroads: without the means to maintain its galactic empire, it must fragment.

Earth leads an alliance of planets on a mission to explore the Quadrangle, an unknown region of space that may hold the secret to restoring her former glory. The crew of the *Paradigm* may be unorthodox, but they've come through the Crisis as heroes. Will former v museum curator Vanderbeam's new role as captain help him forget Princess Jovia, the object of desire assassinated by the architects of the Crisis? What secrets does the Quadrangle hold for mankind? *Will there be a third question?*

CUTTER?! HOW --
KATARAKIS BROKE FREE AND I ESCAPED IN THE CONFUSION! WHAT'S --
JUPITER BOMB DETONATION IN 10 SECONDS. 9. 8.
7. 6. 5.
DO NOT WORRY, SIR. ALL THE SHAKING IS MERELY A METHOD FOR MIXING DRINKS.
SEEMS WASTEFUL, BUT EFFECTIVE.
STRAUB
4. 3. 2.
STARSLIP DRIVE ACTIVATING --
FATE, YOU TEMPESTUOUS --
1.

PRIMARY STARSLIP POWER

CLAP
CLAP
CLAP
THANK YOU, ENGINEER HOLIDAY, FOR DOING THE HONORS!
WE FACE MANY CHALLENGES, BUT LET THIS USHER IN A NEW ERA FOR ALL PLANETS!
CLAP
CLAP
CLAP

WHAT... WHAT ARE WE DOING HERE, EXACTLY? DID WE ESCAPE THE BOMB?
I... WOULD ASSUME?
CLAP CLAP CLAP CLAP CLAP

WHAT ARE THESE GUYS APPLAUDING? THAT HOLIDAY KNOWS HOW TO THROW A SWITCH?
WE'LL RESOLVE IT LATER. FOR NOW, PRETEND WE'RE PROUD OF HER.

WITHOUT STARSLIP DRIVE, ALL PEOPLES CAN FINALLY FORGE A NEW PATH THROUGH THE STARS.
LET'S CONTINUE ON TO THE LIBRIOTRON WHERE WE'LL SEE HOW SUPERLINEAR DRIVE
WHAT THE HECK DID WE STARSLIP INTO?

A2-Z, IS THIS CORRECT? OUR CHRONOMETER SAYS THE YEAR IS 3443.
THAT'S... NEARLY TWO YEARS AGO?
A NEW PATH

THE CLOSEST UNIVERSE MATCH WAS ONE WHERE, IT SEEMS, STARSLIP DRIVE HAS BEEN OUTLAWED.
WE WOULD HAVE HAD TO STARSLIP TO THE LAST INSTANT THAT THEIR FUSELI HAD STARSLIP DRIVE.
WE ARRIVED HERE, AT THE MOMENT OF ITS SHUTDOWN.

QUESTION: AM I CAPTAIN?

WAIT -- IF WE'VE TRAVELED BACKWARDS IN TIME, THEN MAYBE JOVIA --
RECORDS INDICATE JOVIA DIED SEVERAL MONTHS AGO.
MONTHS... ?

I'M ACCESSING LOCAL NEWS LIBRARIES.
IN OUR UNIVERSE HER DEATH WAS RULED AN ACCIDENT.
BUT IN THIS ONE, AN INQUEST WAS CONVENED.
THEY UNCOVERED THE ASSASSINATION. THE EVIDENCE IMPLICATED THE MAKERS OF STARSLIP DRIVE.
VON LUCIFUGE INDICTED

STARSLIP WAS FOUND TO BE FLAWED!
IT'S CURRENTLY BEING ABANDONED IN FAVOR OF JUPITER'S NEW "SUPERLINEAR PROPULSION" TECHNOLOGY.
YES! THAT'S EVERYTHING THAT WAS SUPPOSED TO HAPPEN!

NOT ALL OF IT WAS SUPPOSED TO HAPPEN.

AS LONG AS IT GETS THE JOB DONE. HOLIDAY, LET'S SEE WHAT THIS BABY CAN DO.

YES SIR. SUPERLINEAR PROPULSION IS GO.

Superlinear Drive

Superlinear propulsion (or "**starslip**") takes advantage of the principle that the shortest distance between two points is a straight line. Starslip drive merely finds a line that is straighter than straight.

Applied starslip theory

"Straighter than straight" alludes to the concept of "folding the map" from other theoretical FTL systems, but starslip has more in common with "crumpling the map."

Once a destination is selected, its relative coordinates are needed in order to form a mathematical "envelope" around the ship. This envelope is dynamically computed and "faceted," and is never the same twice. Each facet can be thought of as a lens through which the rest of the universe is visible, and it is unknown until the envelope is generated what its configuration will be. Continuing the lens analogy, a given facet may represent a much shorter path to a destination—or a longer one.

After the initial envelope formation, it is refined by computer until a satisfactorily short distance is found to the destination. There is an upper bound to the amount a given distance can be shortened, and this is reflected by a unitless "starslip factor" system that represents the ratio of superlinearized space to normal space.

Starslip arch

Originally conceived for the previous drive technology, the internals of the arch have been replaced by high-energy sequenced monopolar driveplates. These gimballed driveplates can be Planck-manipulated to create and refine a starslip envelope around the ship. The driveplates are composited from exotic metals mined from Jupiter's lower atmosphere, but also occur naturally in other places.

The conversion to the new superlinear form of starslip drive was made much easier by the reuse of the starslip arches. It would have been possible to remove the arch, but having such a large, encompassing structure on nearly every spacefaring vessel made the task of creating driveplate geometry far simpler.

AH, MR. JINX. THE NEW STARSLIP DRIVE IS... LESS CONVENIENT TO SAY THE LEAST.
YES SIR. WE HAVE FOUR DAYS REMAINING BEFORE WE ARRIVE AT CIRBOZOID.
WE USED TO BE ABLE TO TRAVEL THAT DISTANCE IN MERE MOMENTS!

FREE, INSTANTANEOUS TRAVEL ANYWHERE IS NOW A THING OF THE PAST.
WHAT WILL THIS MEAN FOR THE CONSORTIUM?
THE FUSELI?

WE'LL JUST HAVE TO WAIT AND SEE, SIR.

DO YOU WANT TO PLAY CHESS AGAIN, SIR?
NO, NO. IT'S JUST NEEDLESSLY COMPLEX CHECKERS WITH VIOLENT LITTLE ARCHETYPES.

THERE IT IS. THE WORLDSHIP OVER CIRBOZOID.
ARE YOU "DOING OKAY," "SPORT?"
YES SIR.

KATARAKIS DECIMATED MY PLANET. I'M JUST NERVOUS.
KEEP YOUR WITS ABOUT YOU! THIS MAY REQUIRE --
SHUT IT! HE'S ON THE VIEWER NOW!

ATTENTION TERRAN SCUM! THIS IS YOUR FUTURE OVERLORD KATARAKIS.
AS OF THIS MOMENT, MY WORLDSHIP IS POISED TO TAKE CONTROL OF CIRBOZOID.

YOUR CRUISERS ARE HOPELESSLY -- WHAT THE FRIG

WHERE DID YOU GET A PERFECT REPLICA OF THE SPINE OF THE COSMOS?!
IS THAT AN ACTUAL SECOND SPINE? DID YOU GUYS USE TIME?? DID YOU USE TIME.
MAYBE.

FRIG!! END TRANSMISSION!
THE MOMENT OF GLORY HAS COME! CUTTER, BLOW HIS SHIP IN HALF.

JUST BECAUSE HE CAN'T CONQUER EARTH NOW DOESN'T MEAN WE CAN DESTROY A SHIP 300 TIMES BIGGER THAN US.
HIS RESOLVE IS WEAKENED! HE'S DEFENSELESS!

WE'LL FIGHT HIM WHEN THE REST OF THE ASTRY GETS HERE. TWENTY MINUTES, I PROMISE.
JUST ONE SHOT! TRY AIMING AT THAT BIG SEAM.

EXACTLY WHAT WE NEEDED! HERE COMES THE CAVALRY!
BRILLIANT, MR. JINX!
WITH THE SPINE OF THE COSMOS BLUNTED, KATARAKIS HAS NO REASON TO CONTINUE TO EARTH!

COME IN, FUSELI. THIS IS FLEET ADMIRAL HUFF.
GO AHEAD, HUFFS.
GET OFF THE COMM! WHERE'S THE CAPTAIN?

CAPTAIN VANDERBEAM REPORTING FOR CAPTAIN'S DUTY, SIR!
I DON'T KNOW WHAT YOU DID, BUT YOUR TRANSMISSION FORCED THE WORLDSHIP INTO CIRBOZOID ORBIT!
MAYBE I'VE BEEN WRONG ABOUT YOU, VANDERBEAM.

WELL... I COULDN'T HAVE DONE IT WITHOUT CUTTER AND MR. JINX.
MODESTY IS UNBEFITTING A COMMANDING OFFICER.
LOCK THAT DOWN, SOLDIER.

I DIDN'T MEAN TO STEAL YOUR THUNDER AFTER YOU STOLE MY ORIGINAL THUNDER.
THIS BATTLE IS WHAT MADE THE ADMIRAL PROMOTE ME TO WARTIME CAPTAIN IN THE FIRST PLACE!

THIS TIME, OUR SECOND SPINE OF THE COSMOS HAS ALTERED THE COURSE OF HISTORY.
YOU JUST STOLE THE CAPTAIN'S CHAIR!

CUTTER, CEASE YOUR CROCODILIC LACHRIMATIONS! YOU NEVER WANTED COMMAND!
REMEMBER HOW THAT TURNS OUT?
THAT DOESN'T MEAN I THINK YOU'RE RIGHT FOR THE JOB!

WHAT ABOUT MY THUNDER?

VANDERBEAM, LEMME TAKE THE CON! THIS ISN'T A FREEBIE DO-OVER.
I'LL NOTE IT IN THE CAPTAIN'S LOG, MR. EDGEWISE.
WHICH I WILL WRITE.

MEMNON! WHAT ARE YOU TRYING TO PROVE?!
I NEED THIS!

WE'RE TWO YEARS IN THE PAST! EVERYTHING I KNEW IS GONE.
EVERYTHING. IT ALL STARTED WITH JOVIA'S DEATH.
IF I CAN'T CHANGE THAT... THEN AT LEAST LET ME PROVE MY WORTH AS CAPTAIN OF THIS VESSEL.

THE WORLDSHIP IS GEARING UP FOR STARSLIP.
TARGET ITS GO-PARTS AND MAKE EXPLOSIONS.

YOU CAN'T DO THIS.
I CAN DO THIS!

SEE HERE.
THE WORLDSHIP IS UTILITARIAN IN DESIGN, AND THE CURVES EVOKE 33RD-CENTURY GRONVAR ARCHITECTURE, A PLANET UNDER KATARAKIS' THRALL.

THE GRONVARI BELIEVE PLEASURE AND GOOD CORRESPOND WITH EAST AND WEST, WHILE SADNESS AND EVIL OCCUPY NORTH AND SOUTH.
A2-Z, LAUNCH AN H-BOMB AT THE NORTH END OF THAT CHANNEL! IT'S PROBABLY A CRITICAL AREA!

DIRECT HIT. WE HAVE DESTROYED AN ARBORETUM.
YES! FIRST WE CRIPPLE THEIR MORALE!

FIRING CONTROL, TRY THE SOUTH JUNCTION THIS TIME.
ARE YOU TALKING TO ME?
YES, HOLIDAY.
FIRE A CONTROLLED FIRE AT IT.

BDAM
BEEP BEEP BEEP
... I DON'T BELIEVE IT!
TELEM JUST REGISTERED A DIRECT HIT TO AN i-MATTER COOLING STATION!
SOUNDS UNIMPORTANT.
BEAMS, YOU STALLED THEIR ESCAPE!

... I'M TERRIBLY SORRY... ?
NO, YOU IDIOT! YOU DID IT RIGHT! KATARAKIS IS A SITTING DUCK NOW!

SO... I...
YOU DID A GOOD JOB. YOU DID A GOOD JOB BEING CAPTAIN.
I DON'T FOLLOW.

i-MATTER CONTAINMENT FAILING IN THE SOUTHERN HEMISPHERE!
KROOMM
BDAM
BAH! VENT IT INTO SPACE! EMERGENCY STARSLIP!
WE CAN'T!

HOW ARE THINGS GOING THIS WRONG?!
SIRE, THE ASTRY IS HAMMERING OUR REMAINING I-MATTER REFINERIES.
WORLDSHIP POWER WILL FAIL WITHIN THE HOUR.

HOW DID THEY FIND THEM?! WE WERE SO CAREFUL TO HIDE THE WORLDSHIP'S ONE WEAKNESS!!
WHY DOESN'T ANYTHING GO RIGHT FOR ME?
CRITICAL

ALL I WANTED WAS TO ENSLAVE A DESTROYED UNIVERSE OF TORTURED DEAD.

KATARAKIS. YOUR WORLDSHIP HAS BEEN *DISABLED*.
YOU CAN SURRENDER, OR THE ASTRY CAN LAY SIEGE TO IT FOR A COUPLE WEEKS UNTIL YOU LOSE ATMOSPHERE AND DIE.
I'M THINKING.

I JUST WANT TO KNOW ONE THING: HOW? *WHY?*
THAT'S TWO THINGS, BUT I'LL ANSWER BOTH.

HOW? BECAUSE KATARAKIS IS A PREDICTABLE DESPOT IN *ANY* UNIVERSE.
AND WHY? BECAUSE CIRBOZOID *SHOULDN'T BE ENSLAVED.*
... ANY MORE THAN IT ALREADY IS BY ITS OWN CULTURE OF PATHETIC SUBMISSION.

WE *ARE* PATHETIC, SIR. YOU TRULY KNOW US.
YES. YES.

HIB
THINGS MOVED QUICKLY AFTER THAT.

THE FIGHT AGAINST KATARAKIS ENDED BEFORE IT BEGAN.
LITERALLY, IF YOU INCLUDE ALL THIS TIME NONSENSE.

WHEN DEEP TIME ARRIVED TO DEMAND KATARAKIS' EXTRADITION FOR TIME CRIMES, THE CONSORTIUM, FRAIL FROM THE CRISIS, HAD NO CHOICE BUT TO TURN HIM OVER.

DEEP TIME, PLEASED WITH OUR SWITCH TO SUPERLINEAR DRIVE, LEFT PEACEFULLY.
THERE WAS NO WAR WITH THE FUTURE.

BY THEN, OUR FUSELI HAD BEEN EXPOSED BY OUR PARTY GUESTS AS HAVING COME THROUGH SPACE AND TIME.
SECURITY FOOTAGE OF A LIVING JOVIA HELPED SEAL THE FATE OF THE CORRUPT DIRECTORATE. WE WERE HAILED AS HEROES.

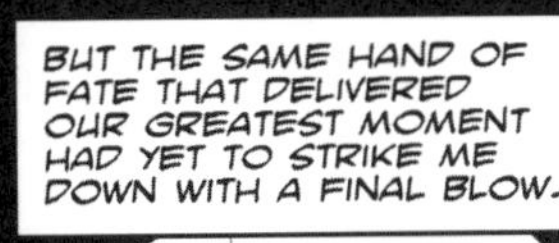
BUT THE SAME HAND OF FATE THAT DELIVERED OUR GREATEST MOMENT HAD YET TO STRIKE ME DOWN WITH A FINAL BLOW.

WEEKS LATER, I FOUND THAT THE TIME SUIT, THE LAST LINK I HAD TO RESCUING JOVIA THAT I HAD SO CAREFULLY HIDDEN, WAS GONE.
OUR PRISONER KATARAKIS MUST HAVE STOLEN IT AND ESCAPED.
I HAVE NOT SEEN HIM SINCE, NOR DO I EXPECT TO.

IN THAT INSTANT, MY JOVIA WAS SEALED AWAY WITHIN THE GRAY VAULT OF THE AGES.

KING JOVOX FINALIZED PLANS WITH THE INTERIM GOVERNMENT FOR A **VOLUNTARY FRAGMENTATION** OF THE TERRAN CONSORTIUM.
TERRAN INTERCULTURE DIRECTORATE
CONSORTIUM IN CRISIS
VECTOR DIRECTRIX
ARTIFICIAL INVESTIGATOR

WITH THE LOSS OF INSTANTANEOUS TRAVEL, EXPERTS SAY THE CONSORTIUM,
WITH ITS HUNDREDS OF MEMBER PLANETS,
IS SIMPLY TOO **LARGE** TO MAINTAIN FROM A SINGLE SEAT OF POWER.

EARTH STANDS ON A PRECIPICE, AND ALTHOUGH THIS CHASM LOOKS FILLED WITH KNIVES AND POISON, I SAY THOSE ARE THE **POISONOUS KNIVES OF HOPE.**
KING JOVOX XVIII
INTERIM GOVERNMENT REPRESENTATIVE

EARTH, CIRBOZOID AND ABOUT TWO DOZEN NEIGHBORING WORLDS WILL SIGN A CHARTER THIS WEEK TO FORM THE **UNITED STAR CONFIGURATION.**
JOVOX IS EXPECTED TO LEAVE HIS THRONE TO BECOME **DIRECTOR** OF THIS NEW ALLIANCE.

MEANWHILE, SAD NEWS FOR HERO CAPTAIN MEMNON VANDERHOFF.
DUE TO RISING FUEL COSTS AND A CHANGING POLITICAL CLIMATE,
THE *FUSELI* WILL BECOME AN **ORBITAL** MUSEUM AFTER ALMOST A DECADE OF SERVICE AS A **TRAVELING** BASTION OF CULTURE.
GOOD NIGHT *FUSELI*

THE *FUSELI* WILL CONTINUE HER SILENT MISSION OF GRACE FROM ABOVE THE SHINING EARTH.
AS FOR MYSELF, I FEEL GREATER THINGS CALLING ME. A DESIRE TO CONTINUE THAT MISSION **HANDS-ON.**
IT WOULD ONLY BE POSSIBLE AT THE HELM OF **ANOTHER STARSHIP.**
MENON VANDYBERM
CURATOR, FUSELI

VANDERHOOT IS REPORTEDLY IN TALKS WITH THE **STARCON ASTRY** TO COMMAND THE INTERCESSOR-CLASS **PARADIGM.**

BY ALL THAT IS **SPACE-HOLY** I WILL KEEP MY PROMISE.
IT'S JUST GOING TO TAKE A **LIIIITTLE** LONGER.

THREE MONTHS LATER, THE UNITED STAR CONFIGURATION SHIP **PARADIGM** WELCOMES ABOARD A NEW CREW.

THIS STOUT CRAFT IS TRULY A **WORTHY** VESSEL FOR MY **DIPLOMATIC SEED.**
MAY IT **CARRY** THAT TRUTH TO A THOUSAND UNKNOWN SUNS! I SAY A **THOUSAND!**

SENIOR STAFF! I'M CAPTAIN MEMNON VANDERBEAM, AND I REQUIRE YOUR ASSEMBLY BEFORE ME.
I SAID **SOME ASSEMBLY REQUIRED!**

OH. YOU GUYS AGAIN.

... DID YOU REALLY NOT KNOW WE TRANSFERRED TO THE PARADIGM, SIR?
I KNEW A THING. SEVERAL, IN FACT.

YOU HAVEN'T EVEN LOOKED AT THE DUTY ROSTER, HAVE YOU?
I LOOKED, AND THE FIRST THING WE'RE DOING IS CHANGING THAT DREADFUL TYPEFACE.
BOLLINGER CONDENSED? PLEASE!

IT'S A SERIF!
LET'S TRY THIS.
HI V-BEAM, I'M CUTTER EDGEWISE AND I'M YOUR TACTICAL LEAD. THIS IS MR. JINX, YOUR SCIENCE OFFICER.

I DON'T NEED YOUR BUSINESS CARD.
WELL, THEY GAVE US A ZILLION OF THEM. THEY'RE AWFUL ROLLING PAPERS.

TELL ME, IS HOLIDAY STILL WITH US?
YUP, SHE'S LEAD ENGINEER. SHE'S BANGING THE PIPES DOWN THERE.

ENGINEERING -- STATUS REPORT.
MERIDIAN LEE HOLIDAY REPORTING IN, CAPTAIN. WE'RE GREEN ACROSS THE BOARD.
DMG

I DIDN'T KNOW YOUR MIDDLE NAME! HOW LOVELY!
MEMNON? YOU'RE COMMANDING ME?
I MEAN, YOU'RE MY CAPTAIN?

I MEAN CAPTAIN OF MY -- THE SHIP, I MEAN. YOUR PARADIGM.
THIS IS THE PARADIGM.
GO ICE SOMETHING DOWN, LEE.

THIS IS THE INFIRMARY, SIR. THE PARADIGM HAS A DOCTOR ON DUTY.
AH! A STEP UP FROM THE FUSELI'S MEDICAL DROID.

CAPTAIN! I'M THE SHIP'S SAWBONES.
GAH!!
I -- FORGIVE ME. I WASN'T EXPECTING... THIS... YOU.

GOOD TO HAVE YOU ABOARD, DOC.
PLEASE, "DOCTOR" AND "DOC" ARE SO FORMAL.

MY NAME IS DAHK TOHRR, BUT CALL ME DAHK.

I'M A MOLIFF. WE'RE SINGLE-CELLED ORGANISMS.
INCREDIBLE! I HAVEN'T YET MET YOUR KIND, DAHK.

IT'S POSSIBLE YOU HAVE AND DIDN'T KNOW IT! WE'RE SHAPESHIFTERS.
OH! FORGIVE ME. THIS IS MY NATURAL FORM.
I CAN SHIFT TO HUMAN TO MAKE YOU FEEL AT EASE.

HHLGLLBLGRGGGHH
UM...

THERE WE ARE! JUST TWO HUMANS, HAVING A CHAT.
OH, NO, IT'S FINE, REALLY. GO... BACK. RIGHT NOW.

C-CAPTAIN VANDERBEAM?
AH. ENSIGNLET. CARRY MY SAUCER AS I TRAVERSE THIS CORRIDOR.
THE DUTY CARPETING IS SCANDALOUSLY UNEVEN.

I'M NOT AN ENSIGN, SIR. MY NAME IS FALTON QUINE, AND I'M THE PROTOCOL OFFICER.
A PLEASURE. BUT I'M QUITE WELL-VERSED IN ETIQUETTE, THANK YOU.

I'M NOT HERE ABOUT ETIQUETTE. THE PROTOCOL OFFICER IS A NECESSITY ON EVERY EXPLORATORY VESSEL, AS SPECIFIED IN THE STARCON CONSTITUTION.
I'M HERE TO ENSURE ADHERENCE TO THE TEN PROTOCOLS.

TELL ME ALL ABOUT IT WHILE YOU HOLD THIS SMALL PORCELAIN OBJECT.

THE TEN PROTOCOLS ARE WHAT GOVERNS THIS SHIP'S INTERACTION WITH NEW BEINGS AND CULTURES.
THEY HAVE TO BE OBSERVED TO THE FULLEST.
I'LL INDULGE YOU, MR. QUINE. WHAT ARE THEY?

I MADE FLYERS.
GOOD HEAVENS. THERE ARE INDEED TEN.

... ZEUS' SPACE-WOUNDS! I CAN'T REMEMBER ALL THIS.
THAT'S WHY I'M ON STAFF. I'M TO ACCOMPANY YOU EVERYWHERE TO MAKE SURE YOU FOLLOW THEM.
EVERYWHERE.

WHAT ABOUT... WHEN I HAVE TO... ?
CASE-BY-CASE BASIS.

The Ten Protocols

Protocol 10 The equality of all sentients must be respected.

Protocol 9 The liberty of all cultures must be protected.

Protocol 8 The privacy of all inhabitants must be valued.

Protocol 7 The security of all citizens must be defended.

Protocol 6 The autonomy of all peoples must be maintained.

Protocol 5 The accountability of all parties must be enforced.

Protocol 4 The defensibility of all accused must be upheld.

Protocol 3 The incongruity of all viewpoints must be reconciled.

Protocol 2 The sanctity of all beliefs must be honored.

Protocol 1 The integrity of all civilizations must be preserved.

A2-Z, ARE WE READY TO GET THIS DURAPLAST STEED UNDERWAY?
AYE CAPTAIN.
TAKE US TO ONE-QUARTER WHATEVER. THE SLOW ONE.

DO YOU MISS THE FUSELI, MR. JINX?
I DON'T MISS MAKING SURE VASES DON'T FALL OVER, SIR.
OH, DON'T THINK THAT I DIDN'T BRING VASES.

THE PARADIGM'S LIGNE CLAIRE DOES HAVE A CERTAIN JE NE SAIS QUOI, BUT I THINK FONDLY OF OUR FINE MUSEUM.
MAY SHE ORBIT IN BEAUTY, SIR.

HOW ABOUT YOU, CUTTER?
I ALWAYS THOUGHT IT LOOKED LIKE A DING-DONG.

WHAT THE SWAMBLE* ARE YOU DOING?
I SPEND A LOT OF TIME ON THE BRIDGE.
* 35th CENTURY CURSE WORD

GUH, YOU CAN'T HANG ART ON THE VIEWSCREEN!
IT'S FOR... DOING EVERYTHING THROUGH.
OH HUSH. I LEFT SPACE BETWEEN THE VERMEER AND THE SHINZON.

INCOMING MESSAGE FROM ADMIRAL HUFF.
I'LL TAKE HIM IN THAT LOWER AREA THERE. THE VIEWING NOOK.

VANDERBEAM! REPORT!

ADMIRAL HUFF! I'M HONORED BY YOUR HONOR.
KEEP YOUR CLOTHES ON, DAGMAR.

I'M ORDERING THE PARADIGM TO A REGION OF SPACE WE COMPLETELY SKIPPED OVER HUNDREDS OF YEARS AGO.
IT'S A 3,000 CUBIC LIGHT-YEAR SPRAWL CALLED THE QUADRANGLE.

TELEMETRY SHOWS A BUNCH OF PLANETS WITH LIFE OUT THERE. GO MAKE FRIENDS.
ADMIRAL, I SENSE A LACK OF ENTHUSIASM.

I'M ALL FOR BEATING SWORDS INTO PLOWSHARES, BUT I'D RATHER DO IT OVER SOMEONE'S SKULL.
MEM
NUH

BEFORE YOU GET UNDERWAY, I WANT THE PARADIGM TO STOP OFF AT CIRBOZOID. MAKE DIPLOMATIC CONTACT WITH THEIR PEOPLE. FOR THE PRESS.
DIPLOMACY! ONE OF MY THREE RANKED GREAT LOVES.

IN THE SPIRIT OF SOLIDARITY, CIRBOZOID IS OFFERING INCREASED TRANSPARENCY.
YOU'LL BE THE FIRST HUMAN CREW TO MEET WITH THE CIRBOZOID QUEEN.
BRING GALOSHES. HUFF OUT.

AH, CIRBOZOID. THAT SHOULD BE A PLEASANT VISITATION FOR YOU, MR. JINX!
YES, SIR. I HAVE MISSED MY COMPATRIOTS.

I DIDN'T REALIZE YOU HAD A QUEEN.
ME NEITHER, SIR.

CAPTAIN'S BLOG, APRUARY 7TH, 3445.
WITH THE CREW SETTLED, WE ARE MAKING OUR WAY TO CIRBOZOID TO BEGIN OUR MISSION OF PEACE, EXPLORATION, AND PERHAPS LOVE.
PROCEEDING AT A VERY REASONABLE STARSLIP SCALAR 4.
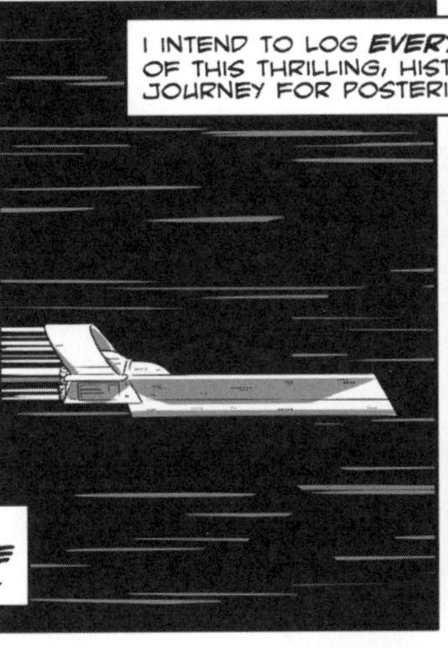
I INTEND TO LOG EVERY MINUTE OF THIS THRILLING, HISTORIC JOURNEY FOR POSTERITY.
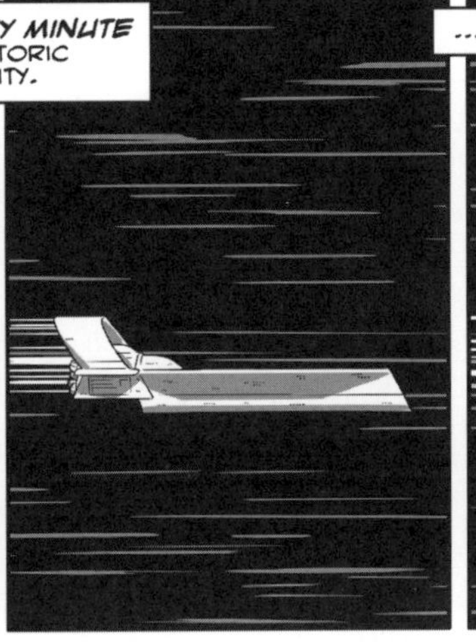
...

REALLY? REALLY. THIS IS WHAT WE'RE DOING?
A2-Z, JUST STOP RECORDI

H-DAY, I THOUGHT DEEP SPACE WOULD BE A RIOT, BUT I GUESS IT'S DIFFERENT WHEN YOU CAN'T INSTANTLY APPEAR AT YOUR DESTINATION.
REMINDS ME OF MY DAYS ON FAR-CORE 7.

YOU WORKED ON A FAR-CORE?
FOR TWO YEARS, AFTER I GRADUATED.
SEEDING SHIFT PROBABILITIES OUT IN THE STICKS. A BANK OF THOSE VIRTUAL MATTER GENERATORS.

I WAS MAINTENANCE, BUT THOSE THINGS NEVER BREAK DOWN.
UGH. WHAT'D YOU DO 16 HOURS A DAY?

STICK MY HAND INTO THE FIELD, AND WAIT FOR THE WAVEFORM TO COLLAPSE ME A COLD BEER.

I ALWAYS FOUND CIRBOZOID BIOLOGY FASCINATING.
YOUR KIND SEEMS INTERESTING AS WELL, SIR.

NOW, STICK OUT YOUR MANDIBULESQUE TENTAPODS AND SAY "AHH."
AHHH.

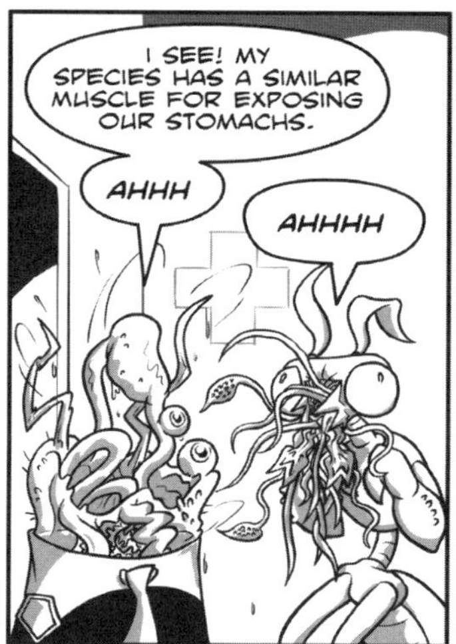
I SEE! MY SPECIES HAS A SIMILAR MUSCLE FOR EXPOSING OUR STOMACHS.
AHHH
AHHHH

I CAN COME BACK.

AH, THE PLANET CIRBOZOID! FREED FROM THAT MADMAN KATARAKIS. GLORIOUSLY FREE!
DON'T USE THAT WORD SO MUCH, SIR. YOU COULD GET FINED THERE.

I SUPPOSE JINX AND I WILL JUST JAUNT TO THE SURFACE VIA SCUTTLEPOD --
REGULATIONS STATE THAT THE PROTOCOL OFFICER MUST ACCOMPANY --
OH COME ON.

CAN'T... COULDN'T YOU JUST ACCOMPANY ME WHERE... BY... BY YOU...

... BEING... DEAD...

IF YOU'D READ YOUR SPEC MANUAL, YOU'D KNOW THE SCUTTLEPODS HAVE BEEN SCUTTLED.
CUTTER! WORDPLAY UNBECOMES YOU.

THIS IS THE NEW AND IMPROVED RELEVATOR.
IT'LL GET US TO THE SURFACE AT CLOSE TO LIGHTSPEED.
WONDROUS!

IMAGINE OUR BODIES BEING DISASSEMBLED AT THE VERY FABRIC OF --
GOING DOWN.

THOOT

Very Deep Space Probability Seed Core

Very Deep Space Probability Seed Cores (or "**far-cores**") are interstellar array stations whose function has deprecated since the advent of superlinear drive. The purpose of far-cores was to "churn" vacuum-contained Eigenstates in order to accelerate the spread of shift drive paths.

Installation of a far-core

A shift drive is used to determine a random path to a point in space. Once up and running, the far-core and its small crew complement activates a series of high-energy serial virtual particle field generators.

Within these fields, every possible common, exotic, conventional and extra-dimensional object appears and is instantaneously annihilated. Eventually, the duplicate of a warship will appear, and an origin ship, can matter-swap places with it across parallel universes. Once a number of highly-ordered objects such as ships have arrived, a stable probabilistic construct forms for other ships to appear within.

Relevator

Still a relativistic elevator, the **relevator** has been refitted to serve transit to a planet's surface. Its speed is roughly 0.1c, making the trip barely noticeable by relevator passengers. Nonetheless, a small percentage of Astry personnel have voiced distaste for the relevator system.

A key element of the relevator is the high-powered momentum softener in the undercarriage, mounted to three ultra-high-impact, J-force solenoidal conductive coils. Without it the passengers would disintegrate upon landing, and the relevator would impact with the force of an atom bomb. The relevator pad is relatively unshielded though, with only a minimal force field to protect passengers from both the vacuum of space and the heat of reentry.

THRSSSHHH
WHKRAM

UGH. I HATE RELEVATORS.
THIS WAS ACTUALLY A LOT SMOOTHER THAN I EXPECTED.
GAH!!

WELCOME TO CIRBOZOID, SIRS. THIS IS CITY OF CIRBOZOID.
THE S-SEAT OF POWER, I TAKE IT.
NO, THAT'S ANOTHER CITY OF CIRBOZOID. WE'LL HAVE TO CROSS THE RIVER CIRBOZOID.

SO... THIS ISN'T THE CAPITOL BUILDING WE JUST PUNCHED A HOLE IN?
OH NO, SIR. THIS IS JUST AN ORPHANAGE.

GOOD SPACE HEAVENS, MR. JINX! WHAT IS THAT?
THERE ARE MANY CASTES OF CIRBOZOIDS, SIR. HE'S A DIGGER.

WHAT CASTE ARE YOU FROM?
I'M A WORKER, SIR. WE'RE THE MOST COMMON.

DIFFERENT CIRBOZOIDS EVOLVED FOR DIFFERENT FUNCTIONS, SIR.
HOW SIMILAR OUR WORLDS ARE!

I SEE MR. QUINE HAS ENCOUNTERED OUR GUARDIAN CLASS.
AUUGH! QUINE! YOUR GUTS!!
THUK!

BY EARTH'S LUNAR MOON! QUINE IS DEAD!
IT APPEARS HE GOT TOO CLOSE TO ONE OF OUR LARVAL SUPPLICATORS.

TO THINK MERE MOMENTS AGO I WAS TIFFING WITH HIM ON THE BRIDGE... !
I NEVER WOULD HAVE WISHED THIS UPON HIM!
BEAMS, I WAS THERE WHEN YOU WISHED IT ON HIM.

SURELY OUR ARGUMENT HAD NOTHING TO DO WITH THIS SAD TURN OF EVENTS!
OH, DIRE IRONY! DIRONY!

OH, QUINE! THERE WAS NO FORESEEING YOUR DEMISE ON AN UNKNOWN ALIEN WORLD.

VANDERBEAM. CAPTAIN VANDERBEAM.
THIS IS HE. WE'VE HAD A TRAGIC ACCIDENT DOWN HERE!

CAPTAIN, THIS IS MR. QUINE. YOU DIDN'T READ THE BRIEFING AT ALL, DID YOU?
QUINE?! BUT... I'M CRADLING YOUR EXQUISITE CORPSE!

THERE ARE ONLY 17 PROTOCOL OFFICERS IN THE ENTIRE FLEET.
WE'RE CONSIDERED SO MISSION-CRITICAL THAT, IF KILLED, OUR MEMORIES ARE TRANSMITTED BACK TO A CLONING TANK ABOARD THE SHIP.
IT WAS A PROGRAM DEVELOPED ONLY FOR PROTOCOL OFFICERS.

SO YOU'RE FINE.
WELL, IT'S UNPLEASANT, BUT --
YAAAYYY.

CLICK CLICK CLICK CLICK CLICK
THE GUARDIANS WILL TAKE US INTO THE ROYAL HIVE TO HOLD COURT WITH THE QUEEN, SIRS.

HAVE YOU EVER MET THIS QUEEN, JINX?
TECHNICALLY, I WAS ONE OF TRILLIONS OF EGGS SECRETED TO A BURROW WALL BY HER OVIPOSITRIX.
LIKE VISITING MOM.

THE QUEEN HAS THOUSANDS OF MALE AND FEMALE PARTS SO SHE CAN SELF-IMPREGNATE AT ALL TIMES.

LIKE... HAVING THOUSANDS OF... DADS...
SORRY, MAN. THERE'S NO WAY TO MAKE THAT PLEASANT.
I KNOW, SIR.

SIR, AS YOU MIGHT IMAGINE, THE QUEEN IS EVEN LESS USED TO HUMANS THAN I AM.
HUSH, MR. JINX. I'M QUITE USED TO DEALING WITH SENSITIVE DIPLOMACIES!

I SHALL ADDRESS YOUR SOVEREIGNTY WITH ALL THE GRACE, EMPATHY AND GENUFLECTION THE SITUATION NECESSITATES!

RIGHT AFTER I PUKE.

GRACIOUS QUEEN OF CIRBOZOID! MY... SINGLE HEART THROBS WITH REVERENCE.

YOUR JUST RULE IS AS FAIR AS YOUR **COMELY FACE**, EYES SET LIKE **JEWELS** AGAINST THE BACKDROP OF YOUR FLOWING **AUBURN HAIR**.

A TOAST TO PEACE! LET US RAISE OUR GLASSES... HIGH.

I PROBABLY COULD HAVE FOUND A BROADER SPEECH TO RECYCLE.
IT'S OKAY, SIR. SHE HAS NO HEARING ORGANS.

CLICK CLICK CLICK
CLICK CLICK CLICK
CLICK
SHE SAYS SHE TRUSTS OUR INTENTIONS.

SHE DOESN'T CLICK LIKE YOU GUYS.
THE QUEEN'S SPEECH IS EXTREMELY DENSE, SIR.

WHAT SHE JUST SAID WOULD TAKE DAYS FOR ME TO RELAY TO YOU IN ENGLISH.
WELL, GIVE US THE GIST OF IT, AT LEAST!

SHE SAYS SHE TRUSTS OUR INTENTIONS, SIR.
THAT WAS ONLY AFTER I TOLD HER I WAS THE CAPTAIN.

HEY, JINX. I THOUGHT THAT YOUR HOMEWORLD WAS A BIG TECHNOLOGY EXPORTER.
IT IS, SIR. WE MAKE ALL KINDS OF DAMPENING AND MOISTENING EQUIPMENT.

ALL I SEE ARE WET ROCKS AND GEYSERS AND A LOT OF NOTHIN'.
MOST OF OUR INDUSTRY IS BELOW GROUND, SIR.

YOU GUYS SHOULD RENT OUT THE SURFACE. LIKE, BUILD A **VACATION SPOT**. MAKE SOME CASH.
THE SURFACE IS TOO POROUS FOR THAT, SIR.

SO, TOO UNSTABLE.
NO, SIR. IT'S POROUS SO WE CAN VENT PRESSURIZED BODY WASTE OUT OF OUR TUNNELS.

I CALL THIS DIPLOMATIC MEETING A RESOUNDING SUCCESS.
A PERFECT TRIAL RUN FOR THE PARADIGM AND HER CREW.

FAREWELL, CIRBOZOID, WORLD OF CLAMMY GRACE!
PARADIGM, THIS IS CAPTAIN VANDERBEAM. THREE GOING UP.

CLICK CLIIICK CLICK CLK CLK CLIIIICKK*
* "I HOPE CAPTAIN JINX AND HIS PETS WILL BE OKAY."

CAPTAIN'S BLOG, SPACE DATE... UH...
HEAVENS, WHAT IS TODAY? IS THIS THWEDNESDAY ALREADY?

YOU SOUND LIKE YOU'RE TRYING TO RECORD A CAPTAIN'S BLOG. DO YOU NEED TODAY'S DATE?
YES, I DO! JUST INSERT IT. THANK YOU.

WE'RE TRAVELING TO THE... WHAT. THIS IS SOME SORT OF SPACE CLUSTER.
WOULD YOU LIKE ME TO INSERT COORDINATES INTO THE RECORDING?
YES.

... ACTUALLY, CAN YOU JUST --
DO THE REST OF IT?
YUP. OKAY. NICE. THANK YOU.

CAPTAIN, WE REALLY SHOULD REVIEW THE TEN PROTOCOLS BEFORE WE ENCOUNTER ANY NEW LIFE.
QUINE, WHAT DOES YOUR LITTLE HANDBOOK SAY ABOUT EARTH BEING THE GREATEST?

IT ACTUALLY TRIES TO AVOID SAYING THAT.
WHAT? BUT OUR ART! OUR CULTURE!
WHAT'S THE PURPOSE OF OUR MISSION IF NOT TO SHARE OURSELVES WITH DESERVING SPECIES?

OUR MISSION IS TO MAKE CONTACT WITH OTHER WORLDS.
PART OF MAKING CONTACT IS LETTING THEM KNOW HOW IMPORTANT WE ARE.

SO CAN WE GO OVER THIS, OR...
EARTH NEEDS A PRESS KIT.

SIR, TELEMETRY HAS PICKED UP AN UNEXPLORED NEBULA.
EXCELLENT!
WALTER BENJAMIN FOR CAPTAINS

GOING INSIDE THERE IS EXACTLY WHAT WE'RE SUPPOSED TO BE DOING.
JINX, LET'S GET A PROBE IN THERE SO WE KNOW --
TSHHH SH SH! MY JOB.

JINX, LAUNCH A PROBE.
SO WE KNOW.
LAUNCHING, SIR.

... ALL RIGHT! LET'S MOVE.
OR, WE COULD WAIT TO GET SOME DATA BACK.
I AGREE. LET'S WAIT.

THE HAVOSH NEBULA IS INCREDIBLY DENSE, SIR, BUT THE PROBE FOUND NO DANGER.
THE GASES HAVE AN ODDLY CONDUCTIVE PROPERTY.
WORTH A LOOK?
IT IS SIGNIFICANT, SIR.

THESE COSMIC VAPORS REMIND ME OF A POLLOCK OR A FRANKENTHALER!
CRIMINY, BEAMS. DOES EVERYTHING HAVE AN ART LESSON BUILT IN?!

OH, PRETTY MUCH.
LOOK. JUST KEEP YOUR EYES OPEN. THIS AREA COULD STILL BE TROUBLE.

YOU DON'T HAVE TO TELL ME.
FRANKENTHALER NEARLY RECONTEXTUALIZED POLLOCK'S AUTUMN RHYTHM.

THIS IS LIKE TAKING THE SHIP THROUGH A BOWL OF PLAVIAN PEA SOUP.*
* SLIGHTLY LESS DENSE THAN TERRAN PEA SOUP, BUT STILL REALLY THICK

GUYS, THE SUBLIGHT ENGINES ARE REALLY HAVING A HARD TIME IN HERE.
WE NEED TO CUT THEM AND GO TO MANEUVERING THRUSTERS.
SYS

WE CAN JUST DO A QUICK SCAN AND DEPART. WE SHOULD PROBABLY HAVE ENGINES.
SIR...

THESE READINGS SAY... THE NEBULA IS ALSO SCANNING US.
GOOD WAY OR BAD WAY?

WHAT DO YOU MEAN, THE NEBULA IS *SCANNING* US?
IT'S AN AMBIENT LOW-LEVEL PROBING SIGNAL, SIR. AND IT'S NOT OURS BEING REFLECTED.

MAYBE THIS BALL OF GAS IS A *LIVING THING!* OPEN A COMM CHANNEL.
ATTENTION GAS. THIS IS CAPTAIN VANDERBEAM OF THE EXPLORER SHIP PARADIGM.

WE COME IN PEACE TO EXPLORE YOUR NETHER REACHES.
IF YOU CAN HEAR THIS, WE MEAN **NO HARM.** WE DESIRE TO ENCOUNTER NEW LIFE FORMS SUCH AS YOURSELF!
IT'S TRULY AN ***HONOR*** TO BE INSIDE YOUR BODY.

NO RESPONSE.
LET'S JUST STOP. PLEASE. RIGHT NOW.

PERHAPS I SHOULD USE MORE *WORDS* --
HOLD THE STAR-PHONE, CAPTAIN. LOOK!

TELEM JUST FOUND A *PLANET*, HIDDEN IN THE NEBULA! IT'S THE SOURCE OF THE SCANS!
INCREDIBLE! A SECRET WORLD TO KNOW!

SPECTROTRON SHOWS BREATHABLE ATMOSPHERE. LIFE SIGNS UNCERTAIN.
VANDERBEAM, I EXPECT YOU TO *LISTEN* TO ME THIS TIME!

YES, YES. I WOULDN'T WANT TO DISTURB THE *DELICATE, UNBUNCHED* NATURE OF YOUR *PANTIES.*
V-BEAM COMING ALIVE! NOT BAD!

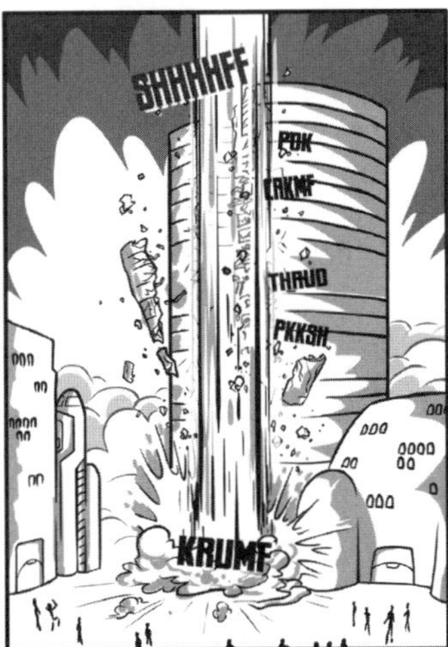
SHHHHFF
POK
CRKNF
THRUD
PKKSH
KRUMF

IT APPEARS THIS PLANET IS INHABITED, SIR.
WE CAN ONLY HOPE THAT, IN TIME, THEY WILL UNDERSTAND OUR WAYS.

CITIZENS OF THE NEBULA WORLD! WE ARE A PEOPLE OF *PEACE!* WE MEAN YOU **NO HARM!**

THKROOOMM

THIS VESSEL SHALL SPEAK FOR IT.
WE'RE NOT AN IT! AND WE'LL SPEAK FOR OURSELVES, THANK YOU.
WE... ?

I DON'T THINK SHE MEANT US. I THINK SHE MEANT HER OWN KIND IS THE "IT."
WELL, LET HER SAY THAT. SHE'S AN ADULT.
WE DON'T KNOW THAT!

I'M GETTING READINGS FROM THESE BEINGS, SIR.
IT'S THE SAME SCAN WAVE PATTERN WE DETECTED FROM ORBIT.
IT'S NOT FROM ANY TECHNOLOGY, BUT FROM THEIR BODIES.

GREAT SPACE HEAVENS! A RACE OF LIVING MACHINES.
THAT... DOESN'T... MEAN THEY'RE MACHINES, VANDERBEAM.
WELL, THEY'RE... OBVIOUSLY VERY WELL CONSTRUCTED --
STOP.

VANDERBEAM, THIS WHOLE RACE HAS PROBABLY NEVER ENCOUNTERED ALIEN BEINGS BEFORE.
QUINE, MAYBE ALL THAT CLONING HAS MADE YOU FORGET. WE'RE HUMANS. THEY'RE THE ALIENS.

I'M MEMNON VANDERBEAM, OF THE STARCON VESSEL PARADIGM.
IT IS QUEL. OF QUELLAR.

THE NEW VESSELS... ARE OF VANDERBEAM...
YET THIS VESSEL... DIVERGES...
I AM A CIRBOZOID, SIR. THE OTHERS ARE HUMAN.

THIS IS SO WONDROUS! WE'RE BRINGING AN ENTIRE GALAXY TO THESE POOR SAVAGES!
I THINK THESE GUYS ARE MORE ADVANCED THAN US.
OH, CUTTER. THEY'RE WEARING BATHROBES.

SHORTLY...
THE QUEL'S LEVEL OF TECHNOLOGY IS NEAR OURS, SIR.
WEIRD. I WONDER WHY WE NEVER RAN INTO THEIR SHIPS BEFORE.

WAIT -- WE DIDN'T DETECT ANY STARSHIPS AT ALL. NOT EVEN SATELLITES.
IT MIGHT HAVE SOMETHING TO DO WITH THE NEBULA, SIR.

THE QUEL BRINGS THE OTHER VESSELS TO ITS COUNCIL.
THESE LINES EVOKE THE POSTMODERN SIMPLICITY OF ERIC MOSS JUXTAPOSED WITH THE WEIGHTLESSNESS OF LATE GEHRY!

HOW THRILLING TO SEE THEIR INFLUENCE IN A CULTURE THAT DOESN'T EVEN KNOW THEM!

THE VANDERBEAM IS NOT OF THE QUEL!
NO, WE'RE VISITORS! FROM OTHER PLANETS LIKE YOUR OWN! AND HOW DID YOU KNOW MY NAME?

IT IS A JOINED MIND. THE VANDERBEAM TOLD QUEL ITS NAME, SO ALL VESSELS KNOW IT.
CAPTAIN, THE NEBULA MUST HAVE INFLUENCED THEIR EVOLUTION. IT'S LIKE AN EXTENSION OF THEIR MINDS!

YOUR WORLD IS SO ADVANCED. WHY HAVEN'T OUR SOCIETIES SPOKEN BEFORE?
QUELLAR PROVIDES ALL FOR THE QUEL. THE QUEL HAS NO INTEREST IN WHAT IS BEYOND THE VAPOR.

BUT YOU HAVE A UNIVERSE FULL OF NEIGHBORS!
YOU'RE MISSING OUT ON ALL KINDS OF SUMMITS AND TRADE AGREEMENTS!

BEHOLD, VANDERBEAM!
QUELLAR HOLDS INFINITE WONDERS. LOOK UPON THE ICE CAVES OF QUOPPOS...

... THE FLAMECHASMS OF AQUINAR...

... EVEN PLACES THAT DO NOT INVOLVE TEMPERATURE EXTREMES TO BE IMPRESSIVE.
THE QUEL IS CONTENT HERE.
BUT... WE COULD LEARN SO MUCH FROM EACH OTHER! ... SHOULD WE LEAVE?

STAY AS LONG AS THE VANDERBEAM DESIRES, EXPLORE AS IT WISHES.
BUT THE QUEL IS NOT INTERESTED IN LEARNING MORE ABOUT IT.
NOT EVEN OUR FOODS?

A FEW DAYS LATER...
AH, CUTTER! MR. JINX! YOU'VE BEEN SPENDING TIME ON THE SURFACE?
MUCH, SIR. THE QUEL HAVE A VERY UNIQUE SOCIETY.

THEY HAVE NO CRIME, NO DISPLEASURE.
EACH KNOWS THE OTHERS' DESIRES AT ALL TIMES.
THEY ARE TRUE EQUALS, WITH ALL HAVING ACCESS TO THE SUM EXPERIENCE OF THE WHOLE SPECIES.

AND THEIR WHOLE CULTURE IS AWESOME. I HAD ONE OF THEIR FOODS -- A BOWL OF DARK PASTE.
BROUGHT A COUPLE BOTTLES BACK.
I'M JUST STUFFED WITH PASTE RIGHT NOW.

GENTLEMEN, I'VE HEARD ENOUGH. ASSEMBLE ON THE RELEVATOR.
WE HAVE TO RESCUE THE QUEL!
SON OF A --

NO ONE IS MESSING WITH THE QUEL! QUINE WOULD HAVE STAR-KITTENS.
BUT THESE PEOPLE ARE SLAVES TO EONS OF EVOLUTION-ENFORCED DOGMATIC IDEOLOGY!

SO... GOTTA SAVE 'EM.
I DOUBT THEY WOULD BE RECEPTIVE TO BEING "SAVED," SIR.
BUT WE HAVE SO MUCH TO GIVE! HOW COULD THEY NOT WANT IT?

ART DIED FOR THE QUEL MILLENNIA AGO BECAUSE THEY ALL KNOW WHAT THE OTHER IS THINKING!
ALL I WANT TO DO IS GIVE THEM A PAINTBRUSH. TO HELP THEM.

TROUBLE ON THE SURFACE, CAPTAIN. THE QUEL ARE REQUESTING ASSISTANCE.
AHA! SEE?! BRING MY PASTELS.

I BROUGHT POETRY. FOR THE PEOPLE.
THE QUEL ASKS THE VANDERBEAM'S HELP WITH THE CYTE.
I'M NOT FAMILIAR WITH HIS WORK.
SHELLEY FOR TELEPATHS

THE CYTE IS A PLAGUE ON QUELLAR'S CITIES. IT HAS GROWN TOO NUMEROUS.
BUGS! LOOKS LIKE THEY'RE ATTACKING A GRAIN SILO.

WHAT DOES THE QUEL NORMALLY DO WHEN ATTACKED?
THE QUEL SACRIFICES ITS VESSELS UNTIL THE CYTE DEPARTS. BUT IT HAS BECOME GREEDY.
SACRIFICES?

WELL, THAT AIN'T HAPPENING TODAY. LET'S HAVE A BUG ROAST.
SIR, PLEASE.
SORRY, JINX. I MEAN, A THOSE BUGS ROAST.

DOES PROTOCOL SAY WE HAVE TO WATCH THESE PEOPLE DIE?
NO, BECAUSE THEY REQUESTED OUR HELP. THIS IS GOOD RELATIONSHIP-BUILDING.
I FEEL SORRY FOR YOUR GIRLFRIENDS.

THESE THINGS ARE BIGGER UP CLOSE! ENGAGE AT WILL!
TEST THEM FOR SENTIENCE! WHAT IF THEY'RE TRYING TO COMMUNICATE?

PAL, THERE'S SENTIENCE AND THEN THERE'S ANGRY BUGS.
THIS AIN'T HELLO!
THIS ONE BIT MY ARM OFF, SIR.

LOVELY!
TELL US, MR. QUINE, WAS THAT "HOW DO YOU DO?" A BOOK CLUB INVITE?
WELL, CHANCES ARE, THEY HAVE NO WRITTEN LANGUAGE.

VANDERBEAM! GET YOUR SIDEARM OUT!
MAKE IT YOUR FRONTARM!
UH... WAIT, ME? HANDLE A WEAPON?

THEY'RE SWARMING! THIS IS GETTING OUT OF HAND!
I'M SPITTING AS FAST AS I CAN, SIRS.
JINX, BE A PEACH AND PARALYZE THEM SOMEWHERE I DON'T HAVE TO SEE IT.

QUINE?? I THOUGHT YOU'D STILL BE TRYING TO TALK TO THEM.
YOU WERE RIGHT, THEY'RE JUST BIG PREDATORY BUGS. PROTOCOL SAYS TO GO ON OFFENSE.
IT'S ABOUT TIME!

OH DEAR.
SHKCHH

THE VESSEL SACRIFICES AS THE QUEL DOES!
WELL, KIND OF.
AND THE OTHER VESSELS... THEY ARE NOT OF THE VANDERBEAM!

OH! MY GOODNESS! YOU MUST HAVE ASSUMED WE WERE A HIVE MIND LIKE YOURSELVES.
EACH OF... THE OTHER VESSELS... IS NOT SHARED?

WE THINK INDEPENDENTLY.
THAT'S WHY WE HAVE CAPTAINS, BECAUSE SOMETIMES WE DON'T KNOW WHAT'S BEST AND HAVE TO BE TOLD.

GENTLEMEN!
CONTINUE FIGHTING!
DEFEND YOURSELVES FROM THEIR SHARPNESS!

I NEED A DRINK.
CUTTER, YOU'VE EARNED IT. COOL, CLEAR WATER FOR ALL!

THE VANDERBEAM AND THE OTHER VESSELS HAVE ASSISTED THE QUEL.
IT BRINGS US PLEASURE TO DO IT! TO HELP OTHERS. A CORNERSTONE OF THE HUMAN SPIRIT!

I'D LIKE TO INVITE AN ENVOY FROM THE QUEL TO TOUR OUR SHIP.
WILL YOU ACCEPT?

THE QUEL ACCEPTS.
OKAY... I DON'T WANT TO BE RUDE, BUT I JUST MEANT ONE PERSON.

THIS IS OUR SHIP, THE PARADIGM.
IT IS A VESSEL FOR OUR **BODIES** IN THE SAME WAY YOUR **BODY** IS A "VESSEL" FOR --
THE QUEL KNOWS WHAT A SHIP IS, VANDERBEAM.

CAPTAIN! NEXT TIME SOMETHING IS ABOUT TO SINK ITS MANDIBLES INTO ME AND YOU'RE RIGHT THERE, **SHOOT IT!**
OH, QUINE. WHY? YOU JUST **RESPAWN.**
IT HURTS! EVERY TIME! ALL THE TIME!

YOUR KIND... FEARS DEATH?
IN DEATH, WE CONFRONT MANY **TRUTHS** ABOUT THE HUMAN CONDITION. IT IS A **CRUCIBLE** IN WHICH WE BECOME TRULY **ALIVE.**

BUT THE SHORT ANSWER IS YES, A LOT.

CAPTAIN, IF WE'RE GOING TO HAVE ONE OF THE QUEL ON BOARD, A **PROPERLY TRAINED** OFFICER SHOULD SHOW HER AROUND.
FINE, QUINE.

HEAVENS. WHAT'S GOTTEN INTO HIS ASCOT?
IS THAT ONE OF THE NEBULA PEOPLE?
WELL, NOT A **PERSON,** HOLIDAY.

QUINE'S WHOLE REASON FOR BEING IS TO MAKE SURE TALKS WITH NEW SPECIES GO SMOOTHLY.
IF HE HANDLES ALL THAT, THEN WHAT DID THEY BRING **ME** ON FOR? OR THIS ENTIRE **CREW?**

WHY NOT LOAD QUINE INTO A TORPEDO AND FIRE HIM INTO UNKNOWN SPACE?
... IS THAT AN ORDER?
NOT YET.

OW. **OW.**
HOLD STILL, CUTTER! YOU'RE LUCKY YOU STILL HAVE LIMBS TO PATCH UP.
LIF

THOSE THINGS WERE FEROCIOUS, DAHK. BUT THEY GO DOWN **EASY** WHEN HIT WITH THE BUSINESS END OF AN **ATOM KNIFE.**
OW!

I DIDN'T THINK A TOUGH GUY LIKE YOU WOULD WINCE AT A COUPLE STITCHES.
LIF

IT'S NOT THAT. I DRANK YOUR RUBBING ALCOHOL AND IT'S MAKING ITS WAY THROUGH MY GUTTYWORKS.

AND THIS IS OUR SUPERLINEAR PROPULSION SYSTEM, WHICH WE CALL STARSLIP DRIVE.
THIS TAKES YOUR KIND BEYOND THE NEBULA?
STARSLIP I

THERE MUST BE MUCH DANGER. BUT THE QUINE CAN REGENERATE.
THE QUINE DOES NOT FEAR DEATH?
I DON'T. I JUST FEAR THE 30 SECONDS LEADING UP TO IT. AS MUCH AS DEATH.

THE QUINE HAS SHARED MUCH WITH THIS VESSEL.
OUR KIND WISHES THE SAME. WILL YOU ACCEPT?
THIS... IS SIGNIFICANT! ON BEHALF OF THE WHOLE CREW, I ACCEPT!

THE ONLY THING BETTER THAN CEMENTING AN ALLIANCE WITH A NEW SPECIES IS SHOVING IT IN VANDERBEAM'S FACE.

GLAD TO SEE YOU TWO UP AND ABOUT.
YES, SIR. MY ARM IS ALMOST FINISHED GROWING BACK.
SADLY I CAN TELL THIS ONE WILL HAVE A TRICK ELBOW.

WHERE'S QUINE? DID HE MAKE IT BACK?
YES, HE'S SHOWING OUR GUEST AROUND.
THAT'S EATIN' YOU UP, HUH.

QUINE IS TRAINED IN THE COLD SCIENCE OF FIRST CONTACT, WHILE I HAVE A POET'S SOUL.
WHEN ENCOUNTERING THE BEAUTIFUL UNKNOWN, NO ONE EVER SAYS, "THEY SHOULD HAVE SENT A SCIENTIST."

SURE THEY DO. THE EXPEDITION TO THAT NOVA, WHERE THEY ONLY SENT POETS TO STUDY IT.
OH. RIGHT. THE "30-SECOND MASSACRE" OF HUTHOK GAMMA.

I WONDER HOW WE'LL RELATE TO THE QUEL AS WE MOVE FORWARD.
AN IDEAL CULTURE SO PERFECT IN ITS ISOLATION IT WANTS NOTHING TO DO WITH WHAT MAKES US US.

WILL WE ALWAYS BE AT ARM'S LENGTH? THEY DON'T EVEN HAVE ART! AND THAT'S MY THING!
BEAMS, QUIT OBSESSING. THE BEST THING IS TO LET QUINE HANDLE THIS.
HE'S ANNOYING, BUT HE'S THE EXPERT.

THERE'S NO SENSE OF TIME HERE! I WONDER IF THIS IS HOW THE QUEL EXPERIENCE REALITY!
SEEMS TO BE FADING NOW... AN ODD LIGHT...

...
OH NO.

HOW DID THIS HAPPEN? WE WERE JUST IN ENGINEERING! DRESSED!!
BUT... THE QUINE ACCEPTED MY REQUEST. TO SHARE.
I THOUGHT YOU MEANT SHARING INFORMATION! WITH YOUR SPECIES!

THE QUINE MADE THIS VESSEL -- MADE ME EXPERIENCE THE UNKNOWN. I COULD NOT PREDICT THE QUINE'S THOUGHTS, KNOW HIS DESIRES.
I HONESTLY DIDN'T THINK I HAD DESIRES.

HOW STRANGE YOUR EXISTENCE IS! I WISH TO KNOW MORE.
STARCON IS GOING TO EAT ME ALIVE! I THINK I BROKE EVERY PROTOCOL IN UNDER...
WAIT, HOW LONG WAS I OUT?!

QUINE! IT'S BEEN SIX HOURS! WHAT HAVE YOU BEEN DOING, LUXURIATING?!
I EXPECT A FULL STATUS REPORT!
GAH!!
QUINE,

SO THE GREAT PROTOCOL OFFICER QUINE IS A REGULAR GOOD-TIME CHARLIE?!
I'M NOT! I DIDN'T KNOW THE QUEL CONSIDER THAT... INFORMATION SHARING.
DON'T USE THAT LANGUAGE ON MY BRIDGE!

AND I LET YOU HANDLE IT YOUR WAY!! I TRUST YOU'LL DO THE RIGHT THING.
I'VE ALREADY FILED A REPORT...
NO! MARRY HER, YOU CAD!

SHE TRIED TO INTERFACE WITH MY MIND, BUT I GUESS IT WAS TOO MUCH FOR ME, AND SHE MUST HAVE... JUST... TRIED... ANOTHER WAY.

I GOTTA ASK. WHAT'S IT LIKE BEIN' WITH A CHICK WHO POSSESSES THE SUM KNOWLEDGE OF HER ENTIRE SPECIES?
YOU SHOULD PROBABLY SEE THE DOCTOR, SIR.

WE RECEIVED YOUR DISTRESS CALL AND CAME AS SOON AS WE COULD.
THE QUEL HAS LOST ONE OF ITS FEMALE VESSELS.

ITS THOUGHTS CANNOT PENETRATE YOUR SHIP. IT ASSUMES THAT THE VESSEL IS BEING HELD THERE.
BUT... SHE'S STANDING RIGHT HERE!

WHAT?! YOU SPEAK THE TRUTH, BUT... THE VESSEL IS SEPARATE TO US! THE QUEL CANNOT SENSE IT!
WHAT HAS THE VANDERBEAM DONE?!

I'M GOING TO COVER FOR YOU, CASSANOVA.
DON'T DO THAT.
WATCH SUPERIOR CAPTAINSMANSHIP MAKE THIS ALL RIGHT.
OH NO.

HONORABLE QUEL -- WE'VE DONE NOTHING TO YOUR "VESSEL."
SHE MADE A CHOICE FOR THE FIRST TIME, AND HELD THE UNKNOWN IN A PASSIONATE EMBRACE!
THAT IS NOT THE QUEL WAY!

IT'S EVERY LIVING BEING'S INALIENABLE HUMAN RIGHT TO CHOOSE!

THIS HAS NEVER HAPPENED BEFORE IN THE HISTORY OF THE QUEL! THE VANDERBEAM AND ITS OTHERS THREATEN QUEL WAY OF LIFE!
LEAVE THIS PLACE! LEAVE QUELLAR!

NO!
THEY SHOWED ME HOW THEIR KIND LIVE AND WORK!
THE QUINE PRACTICED SOMETHING HE CALLS GETTING IT ON!

OUR SOCIETY COULD BENEFIT FROM HUMANS! WE COULD ALL GET IT ON!

THE VANDERBEAM MUST DIE!
ARGGGRKK!
THUKK

IT JUST GLANCED OFF YOUR SHOULDER BLADE, CAPTAIN.
I MET HIS BLADE WITH MINE! UHK! POETIC!

WHY HAS THIS VESSEL COMMITTED VIOLENCE?
I ACTED IN CHORUS! THE QUEL DECIDED THIS TO SAVE ITSELF!
WE MADE NO SUCH DECISION! WE... I...

BEAMS, IT'S CUTTER. WHAT'S GOING ON DOWN THERE?
LIFE, CUTTER! POWERFUL, NAKED AND RAW!
IS QUINE WITH YOU? I'M STAYING UP HERE.

THIS VESSEL HAS ACTED AGAINST YOU IN VIOLENCE, AGAINST THE QUEL'S BELIEFS.
WE HAVE NO MEANS TO PUNISH HIM. TAKE THIS VESSEL AS THE VANDERBEAM SEES FIT, AND LEAVE US.

THIS MAN... HAS DONE NOTHING WRONG.
WHERE YOU ASK PUNISHMENT, I OFFER CONGRATULATIONS. FOR THE FIRST TIME IN HIS LIFE, HE CHOSE AND HE CHOSE ALONE.

I... I DID. I CHOSE TO KILL YOU. I COULD CHOOSE TO KILL YOU AGAIN!
AND I WOULD COMMEND YOU FOR IT.

THE QUEL HAVE SOME SOUL-SEARCHING TO DO. PERHAPS FOR THE FIRST TIME.
CAPTAIN? WE'RE GOING TO LEAVE THEM LIKE THIS?
I THINK YOU HAD MORE TO DO WITH THAT THAN ME, MR. HOT STUFF.

Quel Bleeder Knife

The Quel bleeder knife is a ceremonial blade designed to mortally wound small mammal-like prey animals with one stab. Though the population of Quellar is nearly 100% vegetarian, the Quel have a shared hunting ability related to ancient memories—much like all their abilities.

The small pack mammals, called *rovar*, also possess a hive mind, and are nearly impossible to corner or separate from the rest of the group. Expert Quel hunters would hurl the bleeder knife at a single *rovar*, piercing its sac-like open circulatory system.

The prongs on the hilt allowed blood to flow freely from the animal, effectively killing it with its own pumping heart.

The ancient Quel, due to their own shared mind and own experiences with death, did not perceive this as cruel, but utilitarian. Bleeder knives (or replicas) are commonly kept in council houses as reminders of a more savage past.

WAIT, QUEL COUNCIL -- LET ME SAY SOMETHING.
I'M SORRY OUR FIRST CONTACT WENT SO BAD.
THE QUEL DISTRUSTS THE UNKNOWN, THE QUINE...

... BUT THIS CONFLICT THE QUEL HAS FORESEEN. IN OTHER VISITING SPECIES.
THE QUEL LIVES IN A UNIVERSE OF THOSE UNLIKE ITSELF.
IT CAN NO LONGER PRETEND TO BE ALONE HERE IN THE VAPOR.

IF YOUR CULTURE IS THIS LONG-LIVED, I'M SURE YOU'LL WEATHER THIS STORM.
YES. YES. THE QUEL TAKES COMFORT IN THE PRINCIPLES OF OUR ANCESTRY.

WOOOOOOO!!

CAPTAIN'S BLOG, SPACE TIME WHATEVER.
WITH THE QUEL AT WORK SOLVING THEIR ISSUES, THE CREW IS PREPARING TO SAY GOODBYE TO OUR NEW FRIENDS.

VANDERBEAM, WE CAN'T JUST LEAVE!
I HAVE EVERY CONFIDENCE THEY'LL FACE THIS BOLD NEW ERA IN THEIR HISTORY HEAD ON.

WE NEED TO LET THE QUEL RESOLVE THEIR INTERNAL TURMOIL IN A WAY UNIQUE TO THEM.
TO DO MORE WOULD BE TO INTERFERE.

IT'S AMAZING HOW FAST A COMPLETELY PEACEFUL CIVILIZATION CAN WHIP UP A COUPLE MILLION SHOTGUNS.

THE VANDERBEAM!
YES, QUELSFOLK! I WANTED TO CONGRAT-ULATE YOU ON YOUR FIRST STEPS INTO A LARGER WORLD.
WAIT!

THE QUEL FELT DISCORD FOR THE FIRST TIME... THERE WAS AGGRESSION...
ITS... OUR FACTION HAS CAPTURED THE COUNCIL BUILDING, FOR LACK OF KNOWING WHAT TO DO NEXT!
TEACH US, VANDERBEAM! WHAT DID YOUR KIND DO WHEN FACED WITH WAR?

THERE'S ONLY ONE THING THAT TRULY GUIDED MY PEOPLE. REMEMBER THIS WELL --
WHEN FACED WITH FEAR AND DOUBT... JUST LOOK INSIDE YOUR HEART.

BUT -- WHAT IS A
VANDERBEAM OUT! HELM, TAKE US OUT OF HERE.
SIGNAL DISCONN

CAPTAIN, HOW AM I SUPPOSED TO FILE A REPORT ON THIS MISSION?
QUINE, YOU'LL JUST HAVE TO TELL THE TRUTH.
THAT YOU DID A GREAT JOB.

YOU KNOW, MR. QUINE, I THINK WE GOT OFF ON THE WRONG FOOT.
I THOUGHT YOU WERE JUST SOME POLICY-SPOUTING BUREAUCRAT THAT DIDN'T UNDERSTAND THAT ART AND HUMANITY ARE WORTH THE STRUGGLE.
I AM!!

THEN I THOUGHT YOU WERE JUST SOME OVERSEXED XENO-PARAMOUR.
BUT WHAT YOU DID FOR THE QUEL REALLY TOOK A LOT OF COURAGE.

YOU ARE... REALLY BAD AT ASSESSING SITUATIONS.
PLUS, THANKS TO YOU, WE HAVE A NEW CREWPERSON.
WHAT?!

YOU DON'T FEEL THE LEAST BIT GUILTY ABOUT WHAT HAPPENED TO THE QUEL?
YOU READ QUINE'S REPORT. THERE WAS NO WAY TO KEEP THEM INNOCENT FOREVER.

EVENTUALLY SOME VISITING FLEET WOULD HAVE CAUSED THE SAME CONFLICT WE DID.
OR WORSE, USED THE QUEL'S ISOLATION TO SOME TWISTED END.

BESIDES, THE QUEL NOW TRULY HAVE THE CHANCE TO EXPLORE, TO ACCEPT CHANGE.
I THINK THEY'LL COME OUT STRONGER FOR IT.

AND IF THEY DON'T, IT'S QUINE'S FAULT ANYWAY.
AND WE DON'T LIKE HIM.
NO, WE DON'T.
WE REALLY DON'T.

I HAVE TO SAY, GENTLEMEN, IT'S GOOD TO BE THE CAPTAIN AGAIN.
YOU'RE TAKING TO IT LIKE A GITHORIAN RADFISH TO HEAVY WATER, SIR.

YEAH, I MEAN... YOU ACTUALLY HANDLED THIS WAY BETTER THAN I EXPECTED.
DON'T BE SO SURPRISED, CUTTER.

IT MAY SURPRISE YOU TO KNOW, MY GREAT-GREAT-GREAT-GRANDFATHER, ARGUS VANDERBEAM, WAS A MILITARY MAN.
MAYBE COMMAND IS IN MY BLOOD!

... BEAMS, SERIOUSLY THOUGH. WAY, WAY BETTER THAN I EXPECTED.
DO YOU WANT TO HEAR WHAT I EXPECTED?
NO.

NO MATTER THE DISCIPLINE, THE VANDERBEAMS HAVE LONG STOOD FOR HONOR, JUSTICE AND TRUTH IN THE UNIVERSE.
SO WHAT ARE YOUR POWERS?

TRUTH IS ITS **OWN** POWER.
ALTHOUGH GRANDFATHER WAS **STARTLINGLY** AGILE.
HEY, WAIT A SECOND.

YOU SAID YOUR GREAT-GREAT-WHATEVER WAS A **SOLDIER**. HOW DOES **THAT** FIT IN WITH YOUR PEACEFUL ART AND LEARNING FAMILY?

IT WAS LEARNING AND PEACE WHEN GRAMPY DID IT.

I WAS ENTERING THE QUEL WOMAN INTO OUR CREW ROSTER UNDER "HUMAN RESOURCES -- "
-- WHEN I REALIZED SHE HAS **NO NAME!**

WE COULD CALL HER "QUEL," SIR.
BUT THAT'S THE NAME OF HER **SPECIES!** WE MUST SELECT A UNIQUE NAME THAT WILL FIT HER!
IT COULD TAKE **WEEKS**.

THE SELECTION OF AN EFFECTIVE NAME IS **CRUCIAL**.
PERHAPS WE COULD CALL HER A FEMALE FORM OF **ICARUS**, AS SHE FLEW TOO CLOSE TO **HUMANITY'S FLAME**.
OR **HELEN!** HER BEAUTY LAUNCHED AN INTRASPECIES WAR!

HEY, HOWZABOUT SHE'S A QUEL. SO, RAQUEL. DONE.
YES! I SELECT RAQUEL!
WHAT?! BUT **LAYERS!**

I HAD SOME AFFECTING DREAMS LAST NIGHT. YOU KNOW THE KIND THAT COLOR YOUR WHOLE DAY.
THEY GOOD DREAMS? BAD?

A LITTLE OF BOTH. I DREAMT OF SOMEONE I HAVEN'T SEEN IN A LONG TIME.
I WONDER IF WE WOULD EVER CROSS PATHS AGAIN. SOMEDAYS IT SEEMS INEVITABLE. OTHERS... WHO KNOWS WHERE FATE MAY DELIVER US?

LOST LOVE, EH?
I HAVE DREAMS LIKE THAT TOO. YOU KNOW WHAT? IF IT'S MEANT TO BE, YOU JUST GOTTA BE **PATIENT**.

YOUR DREAM WAS ABOUT BOOZE, WASN'T IT?
WE REUNITE A COUPLE TIMES AN HOUR.

JINX, DO YOU GUYS DREAM?
CIRBOZOIDS DO DREAM, SIR.

THE OTHER NIGHT I DREAMED I WAS A MIND-LESS RESIN SLUG, LEAVING A TRAIL OF GLUE AROUND THE FOUNDATION OF A NEW STRUCTURE.
THEY'RE A COMMON SIGHT AT CONSTRUCTION ZONES ON CIRBOZOID.

AS THE FIRST BLOCKS WERE LOWERED, I QUIVERED IN INSTINCTIVE FEAR.
I LACKED THE INTELLIGENCE TO KNOW THAT, SOON, MY CRUSHED CARCASS WOULD BE A PERMANENT PART OF THE BUILDING.
THEN I FELT THE LAST SLAB BEAR SLOWLY DOWN ON ME, AS MY SAC-LIKE BODY EXPLODED.

WOW, THAT'S SOME NIGHTMARE.
NIGHTMARE?

STARCON LET A COUPLE HOLOLETTERS THROUGH. FROM MY PARENTS.
HOW ARE THEY DOING?

MY FATHER WANTS TO OPEN A HIGH SCHOOL FOR ENGINEERS, SO THAT HE MAY ROB STUDENTS OF NOT FOUR, BUT EIGHT YEARS OF ART.

I ALWAYS FORGET YOU GUYS ARE THE SAME VANDERBEAMS OF VANDERBEAM UNIVERSITY.
IT'S NOT EXACTLY A COMMON NAME.

WHAT'S YOUR HERITAGE?
WE'RE MOSTLY LASER-DUTCH.

DO YOU EVER... GET LETTERS FROM YOUR PARENTS?
NAH. I MEAN, MY DAD TOOK OFF A LONG TIME AGO. MY MOM IS USUALLY TOO DRUNK TO RECORD ANYTHING.

I KNOW EXACTLY WHERE MY MOM IS THOUGH. I GUESS MAYBE I SHOULD SAY HI ONCE IN A WHILE.
SHE TAUGHT ME EVERYTHING I KNOW.
'BOUT DRINKIN'.

JINX, DO YOU EVER GET MESSAGES FROM UGH YOU KNOW WHAT, I'M NOT IN THE MOOD FOR SOME GROSS-OUT HIVE MIND STORY.
ALL EXCHANGING CIRBOZOID JUICES OR WHATEVER.

From Mom
Dear Jinx,
How are you?
????

Dear Meridian,
How are you? Glad to hear you're doing so well after, well. You know. My deepest condolences. It was really good to see the two of you those few months ago. Hector looked happy.

I didn't mean to start with that. I just know it's still on everyone's mind, and I wanted you to know that I'm always here if you need to talk.

I can't imagine what it must be like to lose a fiancé. But with all your family and friends, you'll be all right in time.

With love,
S'yyqtal

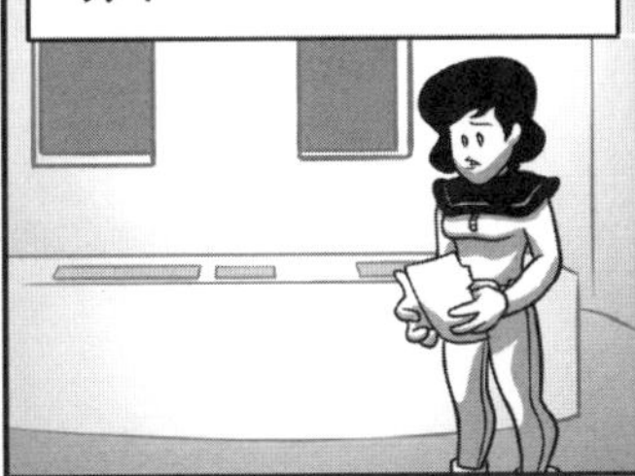

HECTOR ISRAEL O'HARA, AGE 33. FLEET ENGINEER ABOARD THE *EXEMPLAR*.

GRADUATED FROM IRONWEED TECHNICAL ACADEMY IN 3435.

DIED IN A SKIRMISH WITH REPUBLIC FORCES ABOUT SIX MONTHS AGO.

AFTER-ACTION REPORT

BY REQUEST OF FLEET ADMIRAL HU

AH, FAIR HOLIDAY! LET ME BE CLEAR -- BY FAIR I MEAN YOUR FINE ABILITIES AS CREWMEMBER.

VAND -- MEMNON, DO YOU EVER... THINK ABOUT EVERYTHING THAT THE OLD DRIVE SYSTEM CHANGED?
I THINK... THERE'S A LOT OF LIVES IT RUINED. MAYBE A LOT WE DON'T EVEN KNOW ABOUT.

I DON'T KNOW. THEN AGAIN, IT'S POSSIBLE THAT IT ONLY AFFECTED SOME TINY FRACTION.

OR... YEAH...

MR. JINX, DID YOU EVER NOTICE ANYTHING CHANGE AFTER OUR SHIFT?
WELL, THERE WERE ALL THE EVENTS OF THE LAST TWO YEARS, SIR.

I MEANT PERSONALLY. LIKE SOMEONE YOU ONCE KNEW... NOT BEING THERE.
MOST OF MY RELATIVES ARE PRETTY INTERCHANGEABLE, SIR.

I WAS GOING TO TALK TO VANDERBEAM ABOUT IT, BUT HE LANDED ON ME, THEN RAN OFF CRYING.

WHY WOULD HE DO THAT?
WELL, HE SAID HE HAD DROPPED SOMETHING, AND THAT IT HAD SUDDENLY JUMPED INTO HIS EYE.

IF YOUR PARALLEL FIANCE'S PARENTS CONTACT YOU, YOU SHOULD BE HONEST, SIR.
PERHAPS IT'S BEST YOU DON'T DWELL ON IT.
YEAH. YOU'RE RIGHT.

I MEAN... HE OBVIOUSLY DIDN'T WANT ME TO BE UNHAPPY.
IN AN ODD WAY, HECTOR WOULDN'T HAVE WANTED ME TO BE TORTURED LIKE THIS.

HE'S PART OF A PAST THAT WASN'T EVEN REALLY MINE.

I'VE LOCATED AN IMAGE OF HECTOR.
YESSSS

THIS WAS HECTOR.
ARE YOU ALL RIGHT?

... YES. I MEAN... I GUESS I DON'T KNOW WHAT I WAS EXPECTING.

I DIDN'T KNOW THIS MAN. I... I REALLY DON'T FEEL ANYTHING.
I GUESS IT DIDN'T MATTER IF I GOT TO SEE HIM OR NOT.

... PLEASE DON'T LET IT HAVE MATTERED.

HEY. YOU HEAR ABOUT HOLIDAY'S DEAL? IT'S PRETTY SAD.
QUITE.

CAN YOU IMAGINE CARRYING THAT AROUND? UH, I MEAN --
I MEAN... I KNOW YOU TOOK IT HARD WHEN WE LOST JOVIA.

BUT YOU SEEM TO HANDLE IT PRETTY WELL IN THE END. MOVED ON. WE WORRIED ABOUT YOU FOR A WHILE.
YES. WE ALL MOVED ON.

WELL, WE ALL HAVE SOMETHING LIKE THAT.
I LOVED MY EYEBALL, V-BEAM.
BUT NOW I HAVE SOMETHING I LOVE EVEN MORE.
A COOL EMPTY SOCKET.
GAH!!

MERIDIAN, SHED NO TEARS. I CAME TO --
MEMNON, I WASN'T CRYING. I CAN'T.

I SHOULD FEEL SOMETHING, RIGHT? THIS WHOLE THING MAKES ME FEEL SO EMPTY.
MAYBE IT'S A BLESSING. WHEN JOVIA DIED, I WOULD HAVE GIVEN ANYTHING TO FEEL THAT WAY.

IF YOU KNOW NOTHING ABOUT THAT OTHER LIFE... CAN YOU MISS IT?
YOU'RE FRETTING OVER WHETHER OR NOT YOU SHOULD.
THE QUESTION IS, ARE YOU HAPPY NOW?

HEY, JINX.
HELLO SIR. I WASN'T SURE YOU WERE GOING TO BE HUNGRY.
I WOULDN'T MISS OUR SEPTNESDAY LUNCH THING.

IT'S OKAY IF YOU WANTED TO BE ALONE.
NO. I'M DOING ALL RIGHT NOW.

TALKING TO VANDERBEAM HELPED. HE'S BEEN THROUGH THIS KIND OF THING.
JUST KNOWING THAT HE GOT OVER SOMETHING TOUGHER... MAKES ME FEEL LIKE I CAN HANDLE THIS.

THEN LET'S EAT, SIR. I BROUGHT SOMETHING I FOUND CLINGING TO THE UNDERSIDE OF THE RELEVATOR.
I COOKED IT THOROUGHLY.
MAYBE I DO NEED A LITTLE MORE TIME ALONE.

IT'S ALL RIGHT THAT I DON'T GET TO KNOW HECTOR. BECAUSE I'LL NEVER MISS WHAT THEY HAD.
HELL, MAYBE WE WERE MISERABLE. THERE'S NO WAY TO KNOW.

SEVEN MONTHS AGO
MERI!
HECTOR, I CAN'T BELIEVE YOU GOT ENOUGH LEAVE TO SEE ME!
I JUST HAD TO BEFORE I LEFT FOR THE EXEMPLAR.

THIS... THIS IS WHY I CAN LEAVE FOR THIS LONG.
BECAUSE I GET TO COME BACK TO YOU.
I... GUESS IT'S A GOOD THING WE WERE ALREADY GETTING MARRIED, HUH?

I LOVE YOU.
I LOVE YOU TOO.
I CAN'T BELIEVE I'M GONNA BE A FATHER.

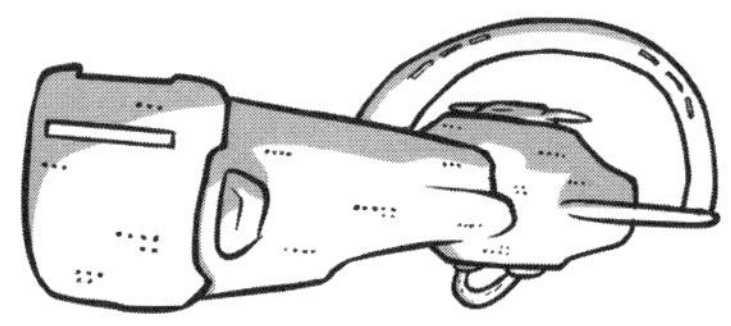

MAN. I'M GLAD THE OLD SHIFT DRIVE IS GONE. IT'LL NEVER CAUSE PROBLEMS AGAIN.
IT'S CAUSED ENOUGH PROBLEMS TO LAST *MANY* LIFETIMES.

BUT I DON'T KNOW, MAN. THE WHOLE "PARALLEL UNIVERSE" THING HAS BEEN A PART OF TRAVEL FOR HUNDREDS OF YEARS.
IT'S KINDA WEIRD THINKING THAT WE'RE STUCK IN *THIS* UNIVERSE. FOR GOOD.
OR FOR WORSE.

DON'T YOU WONDER THOUGH? MAYBE YOU AND I FROM THIS UNIVERSE WERE DIFFERENT.
ONE CAN ONLY HOPE.

SEVEN MONTHS AGO
OH, CUTTER! YOUR *MISCREANCY* ABIDES *NO DEMARCATION!*
RAUSCHENBERG

I WONDER WHAT *MY* PARALLEL SELF WAS LIKE IN THIS UNIVERSE, SIR.
MY THINKING IS, PRETTY CLOSE TO OUR MR. JINX.

I MEAN, CIRBOZOIDS ARE ALL KINDA *SIMILAR,* RIGHT? YOU GUYS DON'T REALLY HAVE A LOT OF VARIETY.
WE... ARE *NUANCED,* SIR.

SEVEN MONTHS AGO

CAPTAIN --
EUGGHHHH.
ARE YOU READY TO DISCUSS THE PROTOCOLS?

NO PRESSURE, BUT THEY ARE THE *TEN MOST IMPORTANT THINGS* ON THIS ENTIRE *SHIP.*
MORE IMPORTANT THAN *PASSION? GALLANTRY?*

VANDERBEAM, *ALL* STARCON CAPTAINS ARE BRIEFED ON THIS THE FIRST DAY, AND YOU'VE PUT THIS OFF FOR *WEEKS!*
THE ONLY THING *I'M* PUTTING OFF IS LISTENING TO *YOU!*
... YES. *THAT'S MY POINT.*

BUCKING "THE MAN" AND MAKING MY OWN RULES.
THIS MUST BE WHAT IT FEELS LIKE TO BE AN ALCOHOLIC.

VANDERBEAM -- I'M ORDERING THE PARADIGM TO A NEW SECTOR OF THE QUADRANGLE.
YOU HAVE NEW ORDERS.

WE'VE DETECTED ADVANCED LIFEFORMS AT THESE COORDINATES.
WE DON'T HAVE A LOT OF FRIENDS IN THE QUADRANGLE, AND JUDGING FROM THESE READINGS, I'D RATHER WE DON'T TURN THEM INTO ENEMIES.

MIGHT I REMIND YOU THAT WE'RE FRESH OFF THE LIBERATION OF THE QUEL WORLD.
AND WE GOT A NEW CREWPERSON TO BOOT.

WELL, HOPEFULLY IN TAKING THE QUEL ON BOARD, WE CAN PROVE TO HER PEOPLE THAT WE'RE NOT SOCIETY-DESTROYING MONSTERS.
SHE'S PROVEN TO US THAT SHE'S A SKILLED CUSTODIAN!

MR. JINX, WHAT DO WE KNOW ABOUT OUR POTENTIAL NEW GALAXY FRIENDS?
THEIR BROADCASTS USE A PECULIAR ISOSPIN RESONANCE UNLIKE OUR SIGNALS.

AND THEIRS ARE SO COMPLEX, OUR LISTENING STATIONS FIRST THOUGHT IT WAS PULSAR NOISE, SIR.
THEY ARE A HIGHLY ORDERED SPECIES, AND APPARENTLY VERY GUARDED.

STARCON HAS DECODED THIS IMAGE OF ONE OF THEM, SIR.
EEYIKES. TALK ABOUT A HATCHET-FACE.

LET'S REALLY MAKE THESE FELLOWS KNOW WE WELCOME THEM DESPITE THEIR APPEARANCE!
DOES ANYONE DO FLORAL ARRANGEMENTS ON BOARD? DO WE HAVE A PERSON?

EXPLORING SPACE IS SUCH COMPELLING WORK!
WE VENTURE INTO THE UNKNOWN... AND BEFRIEND IT.

I REMEMBER THE FIRST TIME I MET HUMANS. IN MEDICAL SCHOOL.
THAT MUST HAVE BEEN QUITE A CULTURE SHOCK.

NOT REALLY -- I'D DONE SO MUCH STUDY BEFOREHAND.
I KNEW I'D BE ENCOUNTERING A RACE OF INQUISITIVE, FRIENDLY SENTIENTS.

COME ON, PEOPLE.

TWO WEEKS LATER
WE'RE REALLY *OUT* HERE, AREN'T WE?
THIS IS THE FARTHEST ANY SHIP HAS EVER TRAVELED INTO THE QUADRANGLE, SIR.

OUR MISSION IS SIMPLE, BUT CRUCIAL.
GET INTO THESE GENTLEFOLK'S GOOD GRACES AND, IF WE CAN, RECRUIT THEM INTO THE UNITED STAR CONFIGURATION AS A NEW MEMBER PLANET!

THEIR WORLD IS ON-SCREEN, SIR.

CAN THEY BE A MEMBER PLANET IF THEIR PLANET ISN'T PLANET-SHAPED?
JINX. CHECK THE BY-LAWS.

DO WE HAVE A NAME FOR OUR AXE-FACED COMPATRIOTS?
WELL, SIR, THEY HAVE A PHRASE THEY USE OFTEN IN THEIR TRANSMISSIONS:
ANTHELERIX POLYGMEON.

WE'VE BEEN SENDING A STANDARD HANDSHAKE USING AN ISOSPIN TRANSCEIVER HOLIDAY BUILT.
SO FAR THERE'S NO RESPONSE.

HONKING OUR HORN AIN'T ENOUGH. I SAY WE FLASH THEM OUR ***HI-BEAMS.***

HOW WOULD WE DO THAT?
SAY HI, BEAMS.
GUH.

A2-Z, PUT ME ON WITH THE ANTHELERIX.
THEY'RE PROBABLY NOT ***CALLED*** THAT. BUT USING THAT PHRASE MIGHT SHOW THEM WE ARE SENTIENT.
YOU GUYS, I MEAN.

ANTHELERIX POLYGMEON! THIS IS CAPTAIN MEMNON VANDERBEAM OF THE STARCON VESSEL PARADIGM.
WE COME IN ***ART.***

HELLO! YES! WE ARE A PEACEFUL, SPACEFARING --

... WELL, THAT WAS RUDE.
MAYBE IT WAS YOUR INFLECTION. I THINK YOU MISSED THE FINAL .
TRANSMISSION DISCONNECTED

THE ANTHELERIX STOPPED ANSWERING OUR COMM REQUESTS ALTOGETHER.
VANDERBEAM... I'M SENSING EMOTIONS.
RAQUEL? YOU ARE??

MY SPECIES IS PRIMARILY TELEPATHIC, VANDERBEAM...
I SENSE... PRIDE... AND FEAR. I SENSE TREPIDATION... BUT A SENSE OF DUTY.

YOU'RE EVEN MORE OF AN ASSET THAN I KNEW! THAT'S INCREDIBLE! THEY'RE JUST LIKE US!

OH, I CAN'T SENSE THE ANTHELERIX. I CAN'T SENSE EMOTIONS BEYOND THIS ROOM.

JINX, IS THEIR... WORLD ACTUALLY A SHIP? IS IT MANUFACTURED?
LIKELY, SIR. IT HAS 1.4 TIMES EARTH'S MASS, BUT IT IS NOWHERE NEAR SPHERICAL.

ARE THERE ANY... DOCKING BAYS OR ANYTHING?
NO, SIR. OR MORE ACCURATELY, BILLIONS.
THE ENTIRE WORLD DOES HAVE A THIN ATMOSPHERE.

HMM. IT'S SO HARD TO LOOK AT THAT THING AND THINK "PLANET."
IT'S NOT LIKE WE ASK FOR DOCKING PROTOCOLS WHEN WE VISIT EARTH. WE JUST LAND.

HELM! PUT US WITHIN RELEVATOR DISTANCE. SHOOT FOR SOMEWHERE NOT TOO POKY.

KREEEEEESSHHH

WAAAUUGGH!

I GUESS -- AAGH -- GRAVITY DOESN'T WORK THE SAME THIS FAR BELOW THE PLANET'S SURFACE!

QUINE, PULL YOURSELF TOGETHER, YOU LOOK RIDICULOUS.

JINX, WHERE ARE OUR IMPROMPTU HOSTS?
IS THIS SOME KIND OF CAVE FORMATION?
STRONG LIFESIGN READINGS NEARBY, SIR. PERHAPS A SETTLEMENT OR CITY.

WE NEED TO STICK TO THE STANDARD GREETING PROTOCOLS. WE DIDN'T GET ENOUGH CONTEXT FOR THE TRANSLATORS.

SO WORDS THAT INITIATE COMMUNICATION, LIKE "GREETINGS" OR "WELCOME" OR --
HELLO.
YES, "HELLO," OR --

HELLO! ANTHELERIX POLYGMEON!
WE SPOKE EARLIER? AT THE THING?
CAN THEY NOT HEAR US? DO THEY NOT HAVE HEARING?

I DOUBT THEY'D IGNORE US AFTER CONTACTING US.
MAYBE WE JUST NEED TO GET IN THEIR LINE OF SIGHT.

DOES THAT MEAN WE NEED TO CLIMB UP SOMEWHERE, SIR?
I WONDER IF THEIR SPECIES CAN EVEN TILT THEIR HEADS DOWN.

EVOLUTION IS *INDEED* A WONDER!
IF *MY* FEET LOOKED LIKE THAT, I WOULDN'T WANT TO LOOK DOWN.

BUZZ BUZZ. GUYS. PARADIGM TO LANDING PARTY.
GO AHEAD, CUTTER. THIS PARTY HAS FEWER GUESTS THAN WE'D HOPED.

OH, DID QUINE DIE AGAIN?
... NO, I MEAN... THE ANTHELERIX AREN'T TALKING TO US.
OH, YEAH. WELL, THAT'S WHAT I'M CALLING ABOUT.

WE JUST CONTACTED STARCON TO UPDATE THEM, AND WHEN WE DID, WE GOT A BROADCAST FROM THE ANTHELERIX AGAIN.
IT WAS THE EXACT SAME MESSAGE. IT'S SOME KIND OF DEFAULT AUTO-RESPONSE.

WHY CAN'T WE JUST ARRIVE AT A PLANET AND BE HERALDED AS KINGS AND HEROES LIKE IN MY DIARY?

I READ YOUR PRELIMINARY REPORT. I UNDERSTAND THERE ARE ISSUES, BUT THE MISSION HASN'T CHANGED.
WE CAN'T AFFORD **NOT** TO BE ON GOOD DIPLOMATIC TERMS WITH THE ANTHELERIX.

IT'S NOT JUST A LANGUAGE BARRIER... THIS IS A SPECIES WITH A FUNDAMENTALLY DIFFERENT STATE OF **EXISTENCE.**

DO YOU HAVE **PROOF** THE ANTHELERIX ARE UNREACHABLE? OR HAVE YOU JUST ALREADY **GIVEN UP?**
MAYBE YOU SHOULD TRY APPEALING TO THEIR BIGGER NATURE.

SIR, ALL THEY'VE **GOT** IS A BIGGER NATURE.

I'VE BEEN THINKING... THE LAST THING WE WANT TO DO IS **TOUCH** THEM.
THEY DON'T EVER TOUCH EACH OTHER, HAVE YOU NOTICED?
I NOTICED THAT **I** DON'T WANT TO TOUCH THEM.

THE ONLY REAL BEHAVIOR WE'VE SEEN IS THE COLUMNS OF LIGHT SHOOTING DOWN FROM THE CEILING ONTO THEM.
COULD THEY BE TALKING? **EATING?** WE DON'T HAVE ENOUGH INFORMATION YET!

MR. JINX, WHEN WILL YOU BE ABLE TO ANALYZE IT?

I'LL ADD IT TO THE LIST, SIR.

I'VE MADE AN INCREDIBLE OBSERVATION, SIRS.
THIS CAVERN, THE FLOOR, THE WALLS... EVEN THE ANTHELERIX THEMSELVES ARE COMPOSED OF THE **SAME MATERIAL.**

IT IS PLANCK-CELLULAR, AND COMPLETELY SELF-RECONFIGURABLE.
THEY CARRY HIGHLY COMPLEX QUANTUM STATES AND PROBABLY STORE UNTOLD QUANTITIES OF DATA.
3-SPACE GRANULARITY

IT WOULD TAKE BILLIONS OF YEARS TO EVOLVE THIS KIND OF MATTER COMPLEXITY.
WE MAY BE LOOKING AT ONE OF THE OLDEST SPECIES IN THE UNIVERSE.

THIS IS WHAT YOU'VE BEEN DOING? WE'RE TRYING TO SAY **HI** TO THEM, MR. JINX.
I'M **VERY** DISAPPOINTED.

IT'S OBVIOUS, MR. QUINE, THAT OUR TRADITIONAL METHODS OF COMMUNICATION ARE INEFFECTIVE.
WHAT WE HAVE HERE IS A **NONFEASANCE** TO **LINGUALLY CONVEY**.

I THINK WE SHOULD MEET BACK ON THE *PARADIGM* WITH OUR SENIOR STAFF AND DISCUSS.
WAIT. WHERE WORDS FAIL, **ART** SHALL PREVAIL!

WHAT'S THE HOLDUP, GUYS? HUFF IS HUFFING DOWN MY NECK OVER THIS.
THE ANTHELERIX AREN'T VERY **RESULTS-ORIENTED**.

DID YOU TRY GETTING UP IN THEIR EYELINE? HECK, MAYBE THESE GUYS ARE THE ANTHELERIX'S **PETS** --

UH...
HUP

DID... THEY JUST SHOW US THE **DOOR?**

WE'RE ON THE VERGE OF SOMETHING **ENORMOUS**.

THE ANTHELERIX SEEM TO HAVE THE TECHNOLOGY TO SEND A CRAFT COUNTLESS LIGHT YEARS AWAY WITH PINPOINT PRECISION.
WITH THAT ABILITY, WE COULD **EASILY** RESTORE THE OLD CONSORTIUM.*
* THE OLD EARTH EMPIRE THAT EXISTED WHEN SHIFT DRIVE WASN'T ILLEGAL.

IF HAVING THE ANTHELERIX AS OUR ALLIES WAS A GOOD IDEA BEFORE, IT'S **IMPERATIVE** NOW.
WHAT DO YOU WANT US TO DO, TRUCK BACK OUT THERE? IT TOOK **WEEKS!**

I THINK WE BOTH KNOW WHAT THE ADMIRAL MEANS.
SIGH BRINGING ALONG BOOKS WITHOUT PICTURES IN THEM.

MAKING THIS LONG TREK AGAIN GIVES US AN ADVANTAGE, QUINE!
YOU NOW HAVE TIME TO LEARN THE ANTHELERIX LANGUAGE!

MASTERY OF ITS NUANCED IDIOSYNCRASIES IS ESSENTIAL TO OUR POTENTIAL ALLIANCE!
THANKFULLY, A2-Z HAS DOWNLOADED ASTRY LINGUISTS' ANALYSIS OF THEIR VOCAL PATTERNS.

I WISH WE COULD BE MORE SURE THAT --
YOUR LESSON BEGINS NOW!

FIRST, HAVE TWENTY-THREE METER-LONG RADIAL TONGUES.
I'LL WAIT.

WE'VE BROKEN DOWN THE ANTHELERIX MESSAGE INTO 148 COMPONENT PHONEMES.
YOU ONLY NEED TO USE THIRTY-THREE OF THEM.

DO WE KNOW WHAT THE WELCOME MESSAGE SAID?
A LOT OF IT WAS RAW DATA. WE THINK IT WAS MEASUREMENTS OF THEIR BIOLOGY. HEIGHT, WEIGHT, THAT STUFF.

THAT SOUNDS PROMISING!
THERE WAS ONLY ONE CONTEXTUAL THREAD THAT WE FOUND, THOUGH.

WHAT DID IT SAY?
"WE ARE LEARNERS. YOU ARE INTERRUPTERS."

WEEKS LATER
LET'S HOPE THIS WORKS, QUINE. ALL OUR HOPES OF MAKING AN IMPRESSION ON THESE GUYS RESTS ON YOU.

THE SAME LIGHT THEY USE! GOOD WORK, QUINE!

I DON'T KNOW, THIS FEELS... A LITTLE...

OH, QUINE.

I THINK QUINE MESSED UP, OR THESE GUYS REALLY WANT TO BE LEFT ALONE.
... WHY IS IT STILL LOOKING AT US?

OTHERS ARE WANDERING OVER! THIS CAN'T BE GOOD!

I CERTAINLY HOPE THEY AT LEAST USE A MORE CAPTAINLY BEAM TO DESTROY ME.

THIS AGAIN?! I THINK THE ANTHELERIX HAVE MADE THEIR STANCE CLEAR AT THIS POINT.
PARADIGM, THIS IS ADMIRAL HUFF!

FAILURE IS NOT AN OPTION!
YOU WILL IMMEDIATELY SHARE YOUR FINDINGS WITH US AND BEGIN THE STARSLIP BACK TO THE ANTHELERIX!

SIR... TELEMETRY SHOWS... ALL OUR STAR CHARTS ARE VASTLY INCORRECT.
YET... ALL KNOWN STAR SYSTEMS ARE SHOWING CORRECT COORDINATES RELATIVE TO US.

THE ANTHELERIX MADE THEIR STANCE A LITTLE TOO CLEAR.

WHAT DID THE ANTHELERIX DO?! DOES THIS AFFECT THE ENTIRE UNITED STAR CONFIGURATION?!
IT APPEARS SO, SIR.

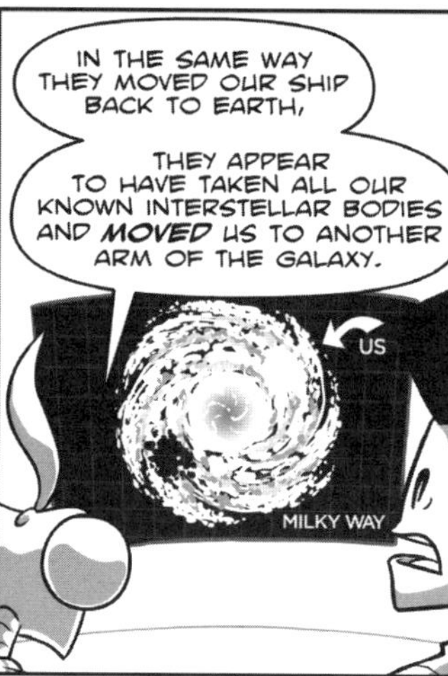

IN THE SAME WAY THEY MOVED OUR SHIP BACK TO EARTH,
THEY APPEAR TO HAVE TAKEN ALL OUR KNOWN INTERSTELLAR BODIES AND MOVED US TO ANOTHER ARM OF THE GALAXY.
US
MILKY WAY

WHERE ARE THE ANTHELERIX?
PRESUMABLY WHERE THEY WERE BEFORE, SIR. BUT IT'S MUCH TOO FAR AWAY TO SCAN, SIR, LET ALONE REACH.

W-WE'LL FIX THIS. SEND A PRIORITY ONE DINNER INVITE. MAYBE WE CAN HASH THIS OUT OVER A GOOD MEAL.
QUINE CAN'T COME.

WORD TRAVELS QUICKLY TO A BEWILDERED POPULACE OF BILLIONS!
STARCON SCIENTISTS AGREE:
WE MUST RELEARN THE STARS
ALIEN RACE TRANSPORTS ALL STAR SYSTEMS TO DISTANT QUADRANT
United Star Configuration scientists have formally released their findings regarding the incident popularly known as the "Starswap Crisis."
A species known as the Anthelerix Polygmeon, unprovoked, used an advanced method of spatial displacement to move the entire network
Rendering of our galaxy

Y'KNOW, I'VE BEEN THINKING ABOUT HOW THIS IS A GOOD THING.
MY SHIP, UNDER MY COMMAND, IS RESPONSIBLE FOR A MIND-BOGGLING RIFT IN ALL SCIENCE. FOREVER.
HOW IS THIS GOOD.

WELL... THERE'S A LOT MORE TO EXPLORE NOW. NEW, UNTAPPED RESOURCES.
ALL THE PLANETS WE KNOW ARE STILL THE SAME DISTANCES FROM EACH OTHER.
ALL WE HAVE TO DO IS UPDATE OUR STAR CHARTS AND IT'S ALL GRAVY.

HOW DRUNK ARE YOU?
I STARTED AT 6 AM. I'M TERRIFIED.

EARTH, A MONTH LATER
THE "NEW SKY" INITIATIVE IS EXCEEDING ALL OUR PROJECTIONS.
WE PREDICT A FULL RECOVERY FROM THE LOSS OF OUR KNOWN CONSTELLATIONS.
TURNS OUT A LOT OF STUFF LOOKS LIKE THE BIG DIPPER.

WONDERFUL TO HEAR. NEXT ON THE AGENDA: EXPLORING OUR NEW ARM OF THE GALAXY.
UNITED STAR CONFIGURATION
OFFICE OF THE DIRECTOR

THERE'S SOMEONE ON LINE THREE FOR YOU, YOUR DIRECTORSHIP.
HE SAYS HE'S GOT SOMETHING YOU'LL WANT TO HEAR ABOUT.
DISCONNECT AT ONCE. WE DON'T CONSULT WITH CRIMINALS.

OH, KINGY.
THE DIRECTORATE USED TO MAKE SO MUCH TIME FOR ME.
I THINK YOU SHOULD CLEAR YOUR DAYPLANNER.

RAQUEL, ARE YOU SATISFIED WITH SWEEPING UP? WE GOT ROBOTS TO DO THAT.
I WANT TO LEARN AS MUCH ABOUT YOUR KIND AS I CAN.

YOU'RE NOT GOING TO LEARN ABOUT BEING A HUMAN BY CLEANING THINGS.
THAT'S JINX WORK.

I THINK YOU NEED A HUMAN BESIDES DUMB OLD QUINE AND VANDERBEAM TO SHOW YOU WHAT BEING A HUMAN IS ALL ABOUT.

SO FORGET YOUR DUTY HERE AND LET'S GET WASTED.
"WAY-STEAD?"
OH, GOOD. I'M SURE THAT WON'T GET ANNOYING.

BACK WHEN WE WERE ON A CIVILIAN SHIP, WE HAD A BAR.
NOW THE CREW HAS TO GET ITS LIQUOR ON THE SLY.
I KNOW ALL THE BEST PLACES.

THE ENVIROTUBE COLLIMATORS ARE ALCOHOL-COOLED.
USUALLY I CAN SIPHON OFF A COUPLE FLASKS WORTH BEFORE THE SYSTEM CATCHES THE LEAK.

THE STARSLIP DRIVE'S TERTIARY REACTOR TOWERS ACTUALLY CONDENSE ETHANOL ON THE OUTSIDES OF THE INTERMIX TANKS.
IT'S NOT MUCH -- I CAN ONLY HIT THIS ABOUT ONCE EVERY TWO WEEKS.

AND, IN A PINCH, CIRBOZOIDS ARE LIKE LIVING STILLS.
WE PRODUCE BOURBON AS A WASTE PRODUCT, SIR.
I AIN'T COMPLAININ'.

I'M NOT SURE I'M LEARNING ANYTHING.
COURSE YOU ARE. YOU JUST... HAVEN'T LEARNED ENOUGH YET.

WHY DO HUMANS DRINK POISON?
WHOA! THIS ISN'T POISON. IT'S CAREFULLY CRAFTED BY BOOZE ARTISANS.

ISN'T IT POISON? IT'S ACTUALLY SLOWLY KILLING YOU.

YEAH, BUT ONCE ALL THOSE PARTS ARE DEAD, ALL THAT'S LEFT IS THE STUFF THAT WANTED TO LIVE.

MR. EDGEWISE, I DON'T KNOW WHY YOU INSIST ON SHOWING RAQUEL THE WORST PARTS OF HUMANITY.
THE *WORST?!*

THIS HAS BEEN AROUND FOR *TEN THOUSAND YEARS!*
IT'S A PART EVERYONE SHOULD UNDERSTAND, GOOD OR BAD!

QUINE, I AGREE WITH CUTTER.
YOU'RE *DENYING HER AUTHENTICITY* DUE TO YOUR *PERSONAL PREJUDICES!!*

WOW, DIDN'T THINK YOU'D TAKE MY SIDE.
I'M NOT. I JUST HATE QUINE.
DON'T GET ANY *REPROBATE* ON ME.

HOW ODD IT IS TO SEE OUR OLD CONSTELLATIONS FROM THIS VANTAGE POINT.
ORION'S FAMOUS BELT JUST LOOKS LIKE A CLOT OF THREE TINY STARS NOW.

CONSTELLATIONS USED TO BE HOW WHOLE *CULTURES* UNDERSTOOD THEIR PLACE IN THE UNIVERSE!

EVERYONE'S GOING TO HAVE TO FIGURE OUT NEW ONES.
ONES THAT REFLECT US *NOW.*

IT'S UNFORTUNATE THAT THIS AREA OF THE GALAXY HAS A LOT OF *BUTTOCKS* IN ITS NIGHT SKY.
PEOPLE CAN JUST TELL THEIR KIDS THEY'RE... WELL... YEAH, THEY REALLY *DO* LOOK LIKE BUTTS, HUH.

AS LONG AS WE'RE AWAITING ORDERS, I THINK MAYBE THE CREW DESERVES A LITTLE SHORE LEAVE.
YOU'RE IN-SYSTEM SO YOU WANT TO VISIT THE *FUSELI.*

NO, I JUST UNDERSTAND THE TOLL THAT REMAINING IN *CLOSE QUARTERS* HAS ON OUR *PERSONNEL.*
PERSONNEL NOTHING, THIS IS ABOUT YOU GOING *STIR CRAZY* ON THIS BOAT.

NO, I JUST THINK THAT YOU'VE EARNED A DAY OR TWO FOR YOURSELF.
DON'T MAKE THIS ABOUT ME. *YOU'RE* FEELING HOMESICK.

WE'RE GOING TO SEE THE *FUSELI* BECAUSE YOU MISS ART AND THAT'S FINAL.
I'M GLAD I FINALLY GOT THROUGH TO YOU.

THERE'S THE FUSELI, AS SHE PROUDLY ORBITS HER MOTHER JUPITER.
SIR, WEREN'T THE ARTIST FUSELI AND THE GOD JUPITER BOTH MEN?

BUT THE SHIP AND THE PLANET ARE FEMALE.
LOOK AT THOSE MAJESTIC CURVES, THOSE SUPPLE CLOUDS!

IF YOU SAY SO, SIR.
YOU'LL LEARN THE NUANCES OF THE ENGLISH LANGUAGE SOMEDAY, MR. JINX.

HELM, PUT US IN ORBIT OVER JUPITER'S PROUD, MASCULINE EYE.
MAY HIS GAZE GRANT US THE FAVOR OF OLYMPUS!

WELCOME BACK, MR. VANDERBEAM.
ASTRID! I TRUST YOU'RE KEEPING MY MUSEUM IN TIPTOP SHAPE!

IT'S A LOT EASIER TO CURATE WHEN THERE ISN'T A WAR ON.
YES, YES. I SUSPECT THE FUSELI WILL EXPERIENCE A NEW GOLDEN AGE UNDER YOUR CURATION!

HER LAST GOLDEN AGE LASTED THE ENTIRE TEN YEARS I WAS CURATOR.
HER ONLY GOLDEN AGE.

... SO SILVER AGE. YOURS WILL BE SILVER.
STILL GOOD. YOU'RE DOING GREAT.

I NEVER THOUGHT I'D LEAVE THIS WORLD BEHIND TO COMMAND ANOTHER SHIP.

I ONCE CURATED ART, AND NOW I CURATE HUMANITY'S PRESENCE IN THE GALAXY.

I WONDER IF ASTRID HAS ANY IDEA HOW MUCH TOUGHER I HAVE IT.

DO WE HAVE ANYMORE OF THESE LEMON THINGS?

MY OLD CURATION OFFICE! I WONDER IF ASTRID IS USING IT NOW.

I GUESS NOT! UNTOUCHED SINCE I WAS HERE LAST!
AND MY **SHIFTED** COUNTERPART HADN'T REALLY SPENT ANY TIME IN HERE SINCE HE **REMAINED** CAPTAIN.

LOOK AT THESE OLD SHOWS I HAD PLANNED.
"LUNAR SEA: THE USE OF WATER IN 22ND CENTURY MOON ARCHITECTURE."
"DESTROYING MICHELANGELO'S DAVID: LITERALLY DESTROYING IT."
"TO MY BELOVED. MY DEAREST MEMNON..."

... JOVIA'S HANDWRITING!
"TO MY BELOVED...?!"

"MY DEAREST MEMNON, I DON'T KNOW HOW MUCH LONGER WE CAN KEEP OUR SECRET."

"I THINK MY FATHER WILL UNDERSTAND OUR RELATIONSHIP -- "
OUR RELATIONSHIP!
" -- AT LEAST I HOPE HE WILL. AFTER ALL, WE HAVE NOTHING TO LOSE."

"WE'LL SEE HOW ARS AD ASTRA GOES. YOU'LL BE FINE."
"AFTER IT'S OVER, COME FIND ME."
"LOVE, JOVIA."
... DATED RIGHT BEFORE HER DEATH.

I'M IN THE RIGHT UNIVERSE AT THE WRONG TIME.

IT'S YET ANOTHER WAY IN WHICH **THIS** UNIVERSE DIFFERS FROM OUR ORIGINAL!
THE **PERFECT** WAY!
JOVIA **LOVED** ME HERE.

I'M **SO CLOSE** TO WHERE I NEED TO BE!
IT'S MERELY THE WRONG TIME!

KATARAKIS IS STILL OUT THERE WITH A FUNCTIONING TIMESUIT.
LAYING **LOW.**
BUT HE CAN'T HIDE FOREVER, AND ONE DAY I'LL --

FINDING EVERYTHING?
TIME! HA HA! FINDING THINGS! HERE'S THAT... DESK. YES.

... AND HERE ARE THE TRANZARK GALLERIES. HE WAS A LESSER IMPRESSIONIST, ONE OF RENOIR'S CONTEMPORARIES.
EXCEPT THAT HE LOOKED LIKE A CRAB.
TRANZARK...

YES, THIS... WASN'T THIS ONE OF YOUR EARLY CURATIONS?
OH. I SUPPOSE IT WAS.
YOU SEEM SO DISTRACTED, MR. VANDERBEAM.

I'M JUST OVER-WHELMED AT BEING BACK ON THE *FUSELI*. A LOT HAPPENED HERE.
I IMAGINE THE REST OF YOUR SENIOR STAFF FEELS THE SAME.

GUESS HOW MUCH BOOZE WAS STILL HIDDEN IN NAVIGATION. ***GUESS.***
DO YOU REMEMBER, SIR?
I SHOULD, I FINISHED IT LAST NIGHT.

ENJOYING YOURSELVES?
YES, QUITE. HOW IS THE IO RESORT?
SULFUR-Y.

WE HAVE NEW ORDERS, CAPTAIN. PLEASE RETURN TO THE *PARADIGM*.
THANK YOU, MR. QUINE. LOOKING FORWARD TO GETTING BACK TO IT?

SO FAR THIS CREW HAS MANAGED TO RUIN AN ANCIENT CIVILIZATION AND ANGER AN EVEN MORE ANCIENT ONE.
I'M HOPEFUL THAT ALL THE EXCITEMENT IS BEHIND US.
GOOD IDEA!

WHAT IS?
HOPING! SINCE INCOMPETENCE HASN'T WORKED OUT VERY WELL FOR YOU.

I HAVE THE MISSION BRIEF HERE, GENTLEMEN.
WELL, READ IT!
YES, READ IT.

LET'S TAKE A MOMENT TO SAVOR THE ANTICIPATION.
LET'S DON'T.
THIS IS SO UNPROFESSIONAL.

IMAGINE TRAVELING TO A NEW, INCREDIBLE DESTINATION. HOPEFULLY SOMETHING WITH TIME TRAVEL!
IMAGINE GOING ON A ***SPEED-OF-LIGHT RIDE.*** LET'S SEE.

"MEDIATE RELOCATION DISPUTE BETWEEN MOLIFF AND SARICAN GOVERNMENTS."
GO BACK TO NOT HAVING READ IT.

SO WHO ARE WE BABYSITTING?
WHEN THE ANTHELERIX MOVED OUR ENTIRE CIVILIZATION TO THIS ARM OF THE GALAXY, THEY MADE ONE SINGLE MISTAKE.

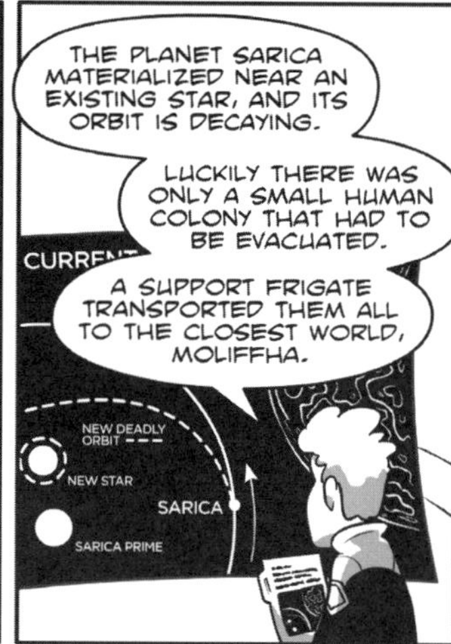
THE PLANET SARICA MATERIALIZED NEAR AN EXISTING STAR, AND ITS ORBIT IS DECAYING.
LUCKILY THERE WAS ONLY A SMALL HUMAN COLONY THAT HAD TO BE EVACUATED.
A SUPPORT FRIGATE TRANSPORTED THEM ALL TO THE CLOSEST WORLD, MOLIFFHA.
NEW DEADLY ORBIT
NEW STAR
SARICA
SARICA PRIME

THE MOLIFF GOVERNMENT ACCEPTED THEM AS EVACUEES, BUT THEY'RE GETTING RESTLESS NOW.
AND STARCON IS STRETCHED TOO *THIN* TO RELOCATE THEM.
SARICA
NEW STAR
SARICA PRIME

SNXXXXX

THE *PARADIGM* IS FAR TOO IMPORTANT FOR THIS KIND OF THING!
ARE WE BEING ASKED TO SERVE AS INTERSTELLAR TAXI?
IT'S NOT THAT SIMPLE.

THE MOLIFF HAVE VERY STRUCTURED DISPLACEMENT LAWS.
THE SARICANS DON'T REALLY HAVE ANY PLACE TO GO ANYWAY. THEY'RE THIRD-GENERATION. THAT COLONY WAS THEIR HOME.

WE'RE BEING SENT TO HELP MEDIATE WHAT COULD AMOUNT TO A POLITICAL ***POWDERKEG*** READY TO ***EXPLODE.***

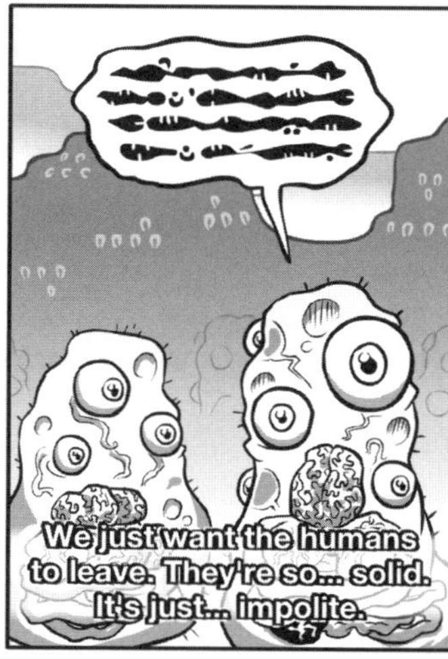
We just want the humans to leave. They're so... solid. It's just... impolite.

The humans were evacuees. They had no choice. Neither did we.

All they do is loiter, all dry and having one shape. It's shameful.

HEY! MOLIFF!

THERE! CHANGED SHAPE!
They also think that's funny.

LOOK, LET'S JUST... POLL THE EVACUEES AND FIND OUT WHERE THEY WANT TO GO, THEN WE'LL --
AND THEN WHAT, **STARSLIP** THEM INSTANTLY THERE? IT DOESN'T WORK THAT WAY ANYMORE!

BESIDES, THE MOLIFF GOVERNMENT WILL ONLY RELEASE THEM TO A PROPER FACILITY.
WELL, THEY CAN RELEASE THEM TO **EARTH!** THEY'RE **HUMANS!**

BY SPECIES, YES! BUT THEY CONSIDER THEMSELVES **SARICAN!**
THEY'RE **ANTI-CRITOCRACY,** WHICH IS WHY THEY LEFT EARTH IN THE FIRST PLACE. THEY'D NEVER WANT TO GO THERE.

DAHK, WHAT DO YOU GUYS... **EAT?**
THAT'S NOT A SOLUTION.

DAHK, I THINK IT WOULD BE BEST IF WE HAD A MOLIFF JOIN US WHEN WE MEET WITH THE GOVERNMENT.
YOU CAN "COUNT" ON ME! SEE, I'M ONE OF YOUR EARTH NUMERALS.
UGH.

AND QUINE... I'M GOING TO ASK THAT YOU REMAIN ON BOARD. THINGS... **HAPPEN** WHEN YOU JOIN US.
I WAS CLEARED BY **TWO** INDEPENDENT INQUESTS!

SEEING AS HOW NEITHER THE MOLIFF OR SARICANS ARE **NEW** SPECIES, WE REALLY DON'T NEED A PROTOCOL OFFICER.
IT'S ALL RIGHT, SIR. YOU CAN JOIN ME FOR MY USUAL ACTIVITIES.

WHAT'S THAT?
STARING BLANKLY OUT A PORTHOLE AT COLD, DEAD, ILLIMITABLE SPACE, SIR.
WONDERFUL, JINX! KEEP HIM OUT OF TROUBLE.

DAHK, BRING US UP TO SPEED ON ALL THE **WEIRD, DUMB RITUALS AND CUSTOMS** OF YOUR PEOPLE.
HONESTLY, MOLIFF CULTURE IS SIMILAR TO EARTH'S IN A LOT OF WAYS!

HOW REFRESHING! MAYBE THIS DISAGREEMENT CAN BE SETTLED QUICKLY!
SADLY, MOST MOLIFF ARE PRETTY PREJUDICED AGAINST SOLIDS.

THAT'S ALL RIGHT, MOST **EARTH-BORN** HAVE A PRETTY DIM VIEW OF THOSE HIPPIE SARICANS.

GENTLEMEN, WITH OUR COMBINED HATREDS, I THINK WE CAN GET THIS DONE IN TWENTY MINUTES.
WHAT SAY? SPORTING BET? **WHAT SAY?**

GRAND HIGH ASSEMBLY, THE PARADIGM IS HERE TO ASSIST IN WHATEVER WAY IT CAN.
PLEASE CLUE US IN ON THAT SOONER THAN LATER.

I'LL BE BLUNT. THE SARICANS HAVE BEEN VERY TOUGH TO PLEASE. THEY WANT TO GO "HOME," BUT THEIR COLONY WORLD IS A CINDER.
PLUS, THEY... MAKE EVERYONE UNCOMFORTABLE WITH THEIR... LACK OF... SHAPE-CHANGING.

I KNOW IT'S CULTURAL AND TOTALLY UNFAIR, BUT IT'S FOREIGN TO OUR KIND.
THEY WALK AROUND, ALL FULL OF RIGID SKELETONS AND... ORGANS THAT EACH DO ONE THING.
DISGUSTING!

... PRESENT COMPANY EXCL... PRESENT... NO, YOU GUYS ARE GROSS TOO.
AUGH! AND THOSE HAIRS!!

CLEARLY A MULTI-PRONGED APPROACH IS OUR BEST BET.
WE'VE GOT TO FIGHT THIS DREADFUL RACISM FROM BOTH SIDES!

CUTTER, I WANT YOU AND THE DOCTOR TO HOST A SERIES OF "SOLIDS AWARENESS" OUTREACH LUNCHEONS.
REALLY? REALLY.

AND MR. JINX, WORK WITH HOLIDAY ON WHERE AND HOW WE CAN MOVE ALL THESE DIRTY SARICANS!

THEY'RE NOT DIRTY, SIR.
PLEASE DON'T LECTURE ME ON DIRTY. I'VE WATCHED YOU EAT.

WHAT DO WE KNOW ABOUT SARICA, SIR?
WELL, THE PLANET ALWAYS FACED ITS SUN THE SAME WAY.
THE COLONISTS LIVED RIGHT ON THE BORDER, IN ETERNAL DUSK.

THE CLIMATE WAS DRY AND COOL -- BASICALLY THE OPPOSITE OF MOLIFFHA. NO WONDER THEY'RE ALL MISERABLE.

EVEN IF WE FOUND A SUITABLE WORLD, THERE'S 650,000 COLONISTS DOWN THERE.
HOW ARE WE SUPPOSED TO MOVE THEM, TREAT THEM LIKE CARGO?

MAYBE WE COULD, SIR. JUST FOR A LITTLE WHILE. WHEN THEY'RE ASLEEP.
SOLUTION FOUND. LET'S PRESENT IT TO THE CAPTAIN.

SO, UH, WHEN WE TALK ABOUT SOLIDS, WE'RE NOT REALLY TALKING ABOUT TOTALLY SOLIDS.
HUMANS CAN BE *REALLY* MUSHY.

ALSO YOU GUYS HAVE EYEBALLS AND STUFF, IT'S NOT LIKE YOU'RE *ALL* SOFT.
I FEEL LIKE I'M NOT DOING A GREAT JOB HERE.

NICE TO SEE SUCH A BIG TURNOUT, THOUGH.
ACTUALLY, COULD YOU GUYS SPREAD OUT? WE'RE TRYING TO GET A HEADCOUNT.

IT'S JUST ME. I'VE BEEN TRYING TO LOSE WEIGHT. *THANKS.*
EEESH.

CAPTAIN! I THINK JINX AND I HAVE A SOLUTION FOR MOVING THE COLONISTS.
EXCELLENT! GO DO IT.

IT'S NOT AS SIMPLE AS THAT. WHAT WE'RE TALKING ABOUT IS BUILDING A FREIGHT *RELEVATOR FRAMEWORK* BENEATH THE CAMP.
KIND OF LIKE HOW THE NIPPON SPACE CONCERN MOVED JAPAN, BUT ON A MUCH SMALLER SCALE.

ISN'T THAT OVERKILL?
IT *WOULD* BE IF WE WANTED IT TO BE SPACEWORTHY FOR MORE THAN A COUPLE MONTHS.
I THINK WITH THE MOLIFFS' HELP WE COULD GET A SIMPLE PROTOTYPE READY IN *WEEKS.*

WELL, I'M ALL FOR EVERYONE ELSE DOING EVERYTHING ELSE FOR EVERYONE ELSE.

THE MOLIFF ARE WILLING TO PROVIDE THE REST OF THE RESOURCES NEEDED TO BUILD THE RELEVATOR!
THAT'S GOOD NEWS, SIR.

NOW THE HARDER PART: FINDING A PLANET *CLOSE* ENOUGH THAT THIS GIANT RELEVATOR WILL BE ABLE TO MAKE THE TRIP CARRYING A HALF-MILLION PEOPLE.
IT EITHER EXISTS OR IT DOESN'T, SIR.

I DON'T KNOW, JINX. EVERYONE SEEMS TO BE HOPING AGAINST ALL *REASON* FOR THIS TO WORK.
AT LEAST *BUILDING* THAT RELEVATOR IS SOMETHING I CAN WRAP MY HEAD AROUND.
I WISH EVERYONE COULD JUST... ACCEPT THEIR DIFFERENCES AND *SETTLE.*

MAYBE CUTTER AND DAHK WILL GET THROUGH TO THE PEOPLE WITH THEIR EDUCATIONAL PROGRAM, SIR.
OKAY, I WANT YOU TO THINK ABOUT WHAT YOU JUST SAID.

CUTTER! DAHK! I'M EAGER TO HEAR OF WORLDS BEING BRIDGED.
THEN YOU SHOULD GO TO A... BRIDGE... FACTORY... CONVENTION.
BECAUSE WE ARE NOT GOOD AT IT.

MOST MOLIFF HAVE NEVER BEEN OFF-PLANET.
KNOWING ABOUT SOLID SPECIES LIKE HUMANS IS DIFFERENT FROM ACTUALLY SEEING THEM GO TO THE BATHROOM.
YEAH -- WAIT, BATHROOM?!

WHEN THE COLONISTS FIRST CAME HERE, THEY WERE JUST AS CONFUSED AS THE MOLIFF.
AS IT TURNS OUT, THE AC VENTS FOR OUR UNDERGROUND BUILDINGS LOOK A LOT LIKE URINALS.

CUTTER! APOLOGIZE ON BEHALF OF THE SARICAN COLONISTS!
BUT I DIDN'T GET TO PEE ON ANYTHING!

WE'VE GOT A TESTBED SET UP ON THE UNINHABITED PLAINS NEAR THE SARICAN SETTLEMENT.

THE MOLIFF GOVERNMENT CONTRACTED WORK OUT TO A COUPLE PRIVATE FIRMS WHO ARE REALLY TURNING IT AROUND IN RECORD TIME.

WHEN WILL YOU BE ABLE TO TRY THE RELEVATOR?
WE'RE DAYS AWAY. ALL THAT'S LEFT IS TO FIND A PLANET TO FIRE IT AT.

MR. JINX --
I'VE ALREADY BEEN LOOKING, SIR.
WITHOUT MY COMMAND?! STOP LOOKING! START LOOKING!

DAYS LATER
LOOK, THE PHYSICS IS SOUND, RIGHT? LET'S JUST FIRE THE RELEVATOR AT THAT UNINHABITED AREA.
IF IT WORKS, WE KNOW IT CAN TRANSPORT ALL THESE REFUGEES AT LEAST THAT DISTANCE.

YEAH. JINX STILL NEEDS TIME TO FIND ANOTHER TARGET PLANET.
AREA'S CLEAR... LET'S GO AHEAD AND CHARGE THE DRIVEPLATES...
SAFETY TEST LAUNCH OF THE FREIGHT RELEVATOR IN 3... 2... 1...

SSSSHHHHHHFHFHFFFFKKTT KROOM

NOW... I'M NO ENGINEER. DID WE JUST SAFELY CRACK OPEN THE PLANET?

WHAT'S GOING ON DOWN THERE? THE COUNCIL MEMBERS ARE OUTRAGED!
I TEST-FIRED THE RELEVATOR, BUT INSTEAD OF BEING RETRIEVED, IT GOT PUSHED FURTHER INTO THE PLANET!
FLX

TELEMETRY SHOWS A WHOLE NETWORK OF CAVES AND SINKHOLES CARVED OUT BY EROSION UNDER THE TEST SITE.
NO ONE WAS HURT THOUGH.

WHAT?! THESE RELAYS WERE MISALIGNED, AND THE THRUSTERS WERE INSTALLED UPSIDE DOWN.
THE MOLIFF CONTRACTORS BUILT IT WRONG!
CRITICAL ERROR

OUR GOVERNMENTS ARE SIMILAR.

INCOMING COMM FROM THE SARICANS, CAPTAIN.
UGH. I'VE BEEN FIELDING ANGRY CALLS FROM THE MOLIFF ALL MORNING!
ON SCREEN. BUT TURN THE VOLUME DOWN FIRST.

CAPTAIN VANDERBEAM, WE JUST WANTED TO THANK YOU, AND IT'S PERFECT.
WHAT IS?
THE NEW SETTLEMENT AREA!

THE NEW CAVES ARE DRY, DIM AND COOL, LIKE OLD SARICA AT TWILIGHT!
WE'VE ALREADY STARTED MOVING OUR HOMES THERE!
I SEE...

CAPTAIN, I'VE BEEN RUNNING SOME TESTS ON HOW WE CAN RESTORE THE CAVE-IN SITE, AND --
SAVE IT.
HELM, MISSION ACCOMPLISHED! FULL STARSLIP!

WELL DONE, CREW! ANOTHER SUCCESS!
REALLY? WE LITERALLY DID NOTHING.

WHAT DO YOU MEAN?
THE SARICANS CAN NOW INHABIT AN ENVIRONMENT THEY PREFER,
AND THE MOLIFF DON'T HAVE TO BE DISCOMFITED BY THE TYRANNY OF SOLID BEINGS.

GREAT, SO, SEPARATE BUT EQUAL.
WELL, IT'S HARDLY EQUAL. THE MOLIFF GET TO ENJOY THEIR SPRAWLING WORLD WHILE THE SARICANS GET A HOLE IN THE GROUND.

... WHICH THEY ENJOY.
WAIT, WHAT'S YOUR POINT.
NEVER MIND, WE WIN.
I THINK WE DID GREAT.

CAPTAIN'S BLOG, SPACE DATE **RIGHT NOW.**
THE *PARADIGM* IS STOPPING AT THE KLIITH OUTPOST FOR STANDARD MAINTENANCE.
I'M TOLD THIS IS **NORMAL** BY MR. JINX.

APPARENTLY DURING SPACE TRAVEL, THE SHIP CAN TAKE OCCASIONAL MINOR DAMAGE FROM MICROMETEOROIDS.
MR. JINX SAID THAT TOO.

THE *PARADIGM* WILL DRY DOCK FOR TWO DAYS WHILE REPAIRS ARE MADE, WHILE THE CREW WILL HEAD STATIONSIDE.
SAYS MR. JINX.

MR. JINX IS STILL EXPLAINING IT TO ME AND THINKS I'M LISTENING.

WELCOME TO OUR FACILITY, CAPTAIN! WE DON'T GET MANY VISITORS OUT HERE.
IT'S AN **HONOR,** MR. RAMDEN! WELL, NOT AN HONOR. A PLEAS -- IT'S NICE. IT'S OKAY.
WE'RE HERE.

OUR TECHNICAL DETAIL IS QUITE FAMILIAR WITH INTERCESSOR-CLASS VESSELS.
UNFORTUNATELY WE HAVE TO ASK THAT THE CREW DISEMBARK DURING THE MORE **MAJOR** REPAIRS.

YOU'RE WELCOME TO STAY ON THE STATION, OR TRAVEL PLANETSIDE TO ENJOY THE WEATHER HORRORS FOUND ON KLIITH.
DOWN THERE THEY HAVE ANTI-TORNADO WARNINGS.

ANTI-TORNADOES?
AREAS WHERE THERE **ISN'T** CURRENTLY A TORNADO.

WHAT ARE YOU TAKING WITH YOU, JINX?
JUST MY CARAPACE WAX. I THINK I CAN GET THREE COATS DONE.
YOU'RE GONNA BE SMOOTH AS A BABY PIRATE'S BOTTOM.

WHAT ABOUT YOU, SIR?
I THOUGHT I'D GET SOME READING DONE.
"DEAD TREASURE: A STAB HILTWARD ADVENTURE."
IT'S A SERIES OF PIRATE DETECTIVE NOVELS.

I READ THE FIRST ONE WHEN I WAS JUST A LITTLE PIRATELET. IT'S **COOL** BECAUSE THE SERIES AGES WITH ITS READERS.

"HIS HYPER-NAUSEA KICKING IN, STAB DRUNKENLY VOMITED THE ATTACKER'S OWN BULLETS BACK AT HIM, EXPLODING HIS FACE-MOUNTED CANNON."
IT'S MATURED A LOT.

ARE YOU TAKING ALL THAT WITH YOU? WE'RE ONLY GONE FOR A DAY AT MOST.
I HAVE A LOT OF PAPERWORK TO DO.

IT CAN'T WAIT UNTIL WE GET BACK?
IF I WAIT UNTIL WE GET BACK, I'LL GET BEHIND.

I'M NOT TEMPTED TO SKIP WORK AT THE *DROP OF A HAT.*
SORRY, THAT'S NOT A COMMENT ABOUT YOU.

IT'S ABOUT THE WHOLE CREW INCLUDING YOU.

MR. RAMDEN, EXPLAIN THE MAINTENANCE PROCESS TO ME.
PLEASE, CALL ME *CRICE.*

WITHOUT YOUR CREW ABOARD THE *PARADIGM,* WE CAN DEEP-SCAN IT TO FIND ANY STRUCTURAL ISSUES.
THEN WE PATCH AND REPAIR THINGS BACK UP TO STARCON FLEET STANDARDS.

DO YOU GET MANY SHIPS OUT HERE AT KLIITH?
IT'S... THERE'S *ENOUGH,* I GUESS.

IT MUST BE DIFFICULT TO STAY *BUSY.*
NAH. WELL, BEFORE YOU ARRIVED WE'D BEEN ASLEEP FOR EIGHT DAYS.

WELL, WITH THE ENTIRETY OF THE CREW OFF THE *PARADIGM,* MAYBE YOU'D LIKE TO VISIT THE SURFACE OF KLIITH.
HONESTLY, I THINK WE'D PREFER TO STAY UP HERE ON THE ORBITAL STATION.

OH, I WASN'T ASKING YOU. I WAS *TELLING* YOU.
YOU START COMMANDS WITH *"MAYBE YOU'D LIKE?"*

WHAT HAPPENED TO THE REAL MAINTENANCE CREW?
YOU'LL FIND OUT WHEN YOU'RE ALL ON *KLIITH.* I THINK YOU'LL FIND YOUR COMMS AND WEAPONS *QUITE* INOPERATIVE.

WE... DIDN'T BRING OURS BECAUSE WE TRUSTED YOU.
YEAH, I FORGOT MINE.
ME TOO.
I NEVER GOT ONE, SIR.

WHERE'S
MY
CREW?
I MEAN, THE 95% OF THEM THAT I NEVER TALK TO?

THEY'RE SAFELY LOCKED INSIDE SOME OF THE OTHER EMPTY DOCKING BAYS.
I'M SURE A STARCON PATROL WILL COME AROUND IN A FEW DAYS. WE'LL BE GONE LONG BEFORE THAT.

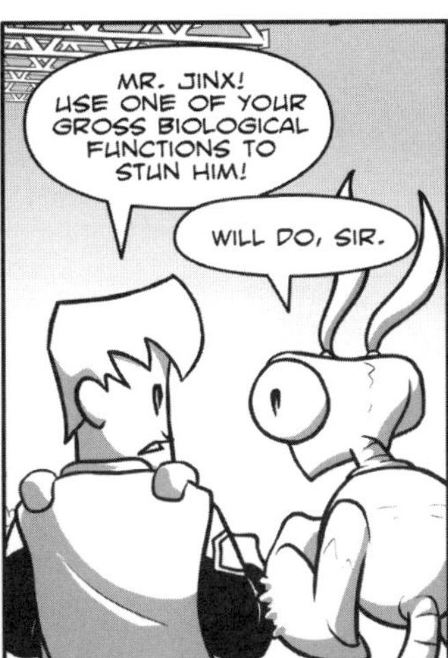
MR. JINX! USE ONE OF YOUR GROSS BIOLOGICAL FUNCTIONS TO STUN HIM!
WILL DO, SIR.

... I MEANT STUN HIM PHYSICALLY, NOT EMOTIONALLY.

LOOK, ONCE YOU DIE, YOU'LL REGENERATE ABOARD THE PARADIGM AND YOU CAN DELIVER THE SHUTDOWN CODES.
MAYBE EVEN GET A LOOK AT WHO WE'RE DEALING WITH HERE.
UGGHHH.

WELL... WHICH OF YOU WANTS TO DO IT?
DO WHAT?
WANTS TO KILL ME SO WE CAN GET THIS OVER WITH?
YOU'RE NOT GOING TO DO IT YOURSELF?!

I DON'T BELIEVE IN SUICIDE --
HERE, WE NEED TO DO THIS BEFORE THE SHIP IS OUT OF RANGE!
THOK

WOW, LITTLE GUY IS TOUGHER THAN HE LOOKS.
THIS'LL TAKE A LOT MORE BEATIN'.

CUTTER, WHY WOULD YOU THINK PUNCHING HIM WOULD DO THE TRICK?
IT USED TO. AGAINST GIANT ANTS. QUINE'S ABOUT THE SAME BUILD.

I'M A DOCTOR! LET ME HANDLE THIS.
WHAT ABOUT YOUR HIPPOCRATIC OATH?
WE TAKE A DIFFERENT ONE.

ACUPRESSURE APPLIED TO TWENTY-ONE POINTS ALONG THE HUMAN SPINE. SHUTS DOWN THE NERVOUS SYSTEM PAINLESSLY.
WOW. I WANT TO LEARN THAT ONE!

YOU DON'T HAVE ENOUGH APPEND -- OH, THAT'S RIGHT, I CAN SHOW YOU.

FWWAAAUUGHH

I MAY REGENERATE, BUT I REMEMBER EVERYTHING.
I HOPE MR. EDGEWISE DOESN'T MIND GETTING WRITTEN UP.

NOW TO GET THESE INTRUDERS OFF THE SHIP.
AS SOON AS I -- OH, COME ON, NO CLEAN UNIFORMS LEFT??
QUINE

BEING NUDE ON STARCON PROPERTY CONSTITUTES A SIMILAR LEVEL OF INSUBORD-INATION.
YOU'RE OFF THE HOOK FOR NOW, CUTTER.

THE PARADIGM HADN'T EVEN GONE TO STARSLIP YET. I'M SURE QUINE GOT ON BOARD.
NOW ALL WE CAN DO IS RELAX.

URRRNT URRRNT
WAIT, WHAT'S GOING ON?
HOLD ON. IT'S THE LOADING BAY CONTROL!

WE'RE INSIDE A SHUTTLE BAY. THIS FLOOR OPENS RIGHT INTO SPACE.
RAMDEN WASN'T BLUFFING! HE'S GOING TO SEND US PLANETSIDE... AS CORPSES!
BAY 6

AND THAT COWARD QUINE HAS RUN FOR THE HILLS!

A2-Z -- EMERGENCY SHUTDOWN CODE QUINE HAWK SNAIL EYE SQUIGGLY LINE THREE FOUR EIGHT.
A2-Z? ...THEY DISABLED HIM.
USCS PARADIGM
UNITED STAR CONFIGURATION
CORE SYSTEM RESTART
If problem persists, contact your administrator.
Error code 0x00AE949716647385

STANDARD PROTOCOL SAYS THAT CAN ONLY BE DONE FROM THE CENTRAL COMPUTER CORE.
I'LL HAVE TO CALL UPON MY COMBAT TRAINING PROTOCOLS.

TIME IS SHORT -- CAN'T WASTE IT TRYING TO FIND CLOTHES.
JUST GET TO THE CORE, GET A2-Z BACK UP, AND THIS WHOLE THING IS OVER.
HECK, MY NUDITY MIGHT EVEN YIELD SOME TACTICAL ADVANTAGE.

I WISH I COULD REMEMBER MY NUDITY PROTOCOLS.

I CAN'T BELIEVE WE GOT AWAY WITH THIS!
THIS WAS THE PERFECT STORM OF PLANNING. THE BOSS IS A GENIUS.

YEAH... BUT... I'M NOT SURE HOW MUCH OF IT WAS THE BOSS.
WHAT? YOU THINK THIS WAS DUMB LUCK?

WELL, LOOK. HOW MUCH OF WHAT HE SAID DID YOU ACTUALLY END UP DOING?
UM. TO TELL YOU, I'VE JUST BEEN WORKING OFF CONTEXT.
THERE'S THE CORE CONTROL CONSOLE, THE TRIPLE-C.
THE STARCON RULEBOOK WILL HELP ME CLEAR THAT ROOM.

THAT'S WHAT I'M SAYING.
I CAN'T UNDERSTAND A SINGLE WORD THAT HE SAYS.
NOW TO FIND... A CAN OR SMALL ROCK TO DISTRACT THEM.

ANYWAY, THE GUY'S JUST WEIRD. IT'S LIKE --
WAIT, WHAT THE HECK IS THAT?
AAAAAAAAAA

AAAAAAAAAA--
DON'T LET HIM HIT THAT OVERRIDE!
WHUK

WHY DO YOU SUPPOSE A NAKED GUY WOULD TRY TO RUN PAST US?
WELL, THERE'S THE CORE OVERRIDE, HE'S PROBABLY A CREWMAN WHO --
NO, I MEAN WHY WAS HE NAKED?

MAYBE HE WAS IN THE SHOWER DURING OUR SWEEP OF THE SHIP, AND --
WWOO-OOP!

GET HIM! HE WAS TWINS!
A2-Z! EMERG MMFFF

WE'D BETTER TAKE HIM TO THE BOSS.
WHAT IF THERE'S OTHERS ON THE SHIP WE MISSED? OR IF HE'S TRIPLETS?

... YOU GUYS SHOULD JUST KILL ME. I'M RELENTLESS AND I'D JUST BE MORE TROUBLE ALIVE!

YOU'RE BUILT LIKE YOUR BROTHER THERE. THAT DOESN'T EXACTLY SAY "RELENTLESSNESS."
"UNDERNOURISHED," MAYBE.

MEANWHILE, IN THE KLIITH OUTPOST SHUTTLE BAY
GOOD SPACE HEAVENS! TO BE BLOWN OUT INTO THE VACUUM AND INCINERATE IN KLIITH'S TORMENTED ATMOSPHERE!
IT BEGGARS BELIEF!

WE WON'T LIVE TO SEE THE PROOF! HOLIDAY!
THESE STATIONS USE OLDER-MODEL QNA INTERFACES. IF THE PIRATES HACKED IN, SO CAN I!

QUICK, VANDERBEAM, TAKE THAT METAL PANEL OFF THE WALL!
INCREDIBLE! I'VE NEVER WATCHED AN INTERFACE HACK BEFORE!

RAAAA
HACK! HACK! HACK!
KRKSHHK

WHY CAN'T YOU UNDERSTAND YOUR LEADER? MAYBE HE WOULDN'T WANT TO SEE ME.

THEY SAY HE'S SUFFERING FROM THE EFFECTS OF PERMADRUNK -- SO MUCH RUM THAT HIS LIVER NOW MAKES IT.
HE FADES IN AND OUT. MAYBE WE ONLY SAW HIM AT HIS WORST.

I'VE READ THE DOSSIERS. I NEVER THOUGHT HE'D BREAK OUT...

INFRA-REDBEARD!
YOU WAS EXPECTIN' SOMEONE ELSE?

I HEARD CUTTER EDGEWISE HAD TRANSFERR'D TO THIS VESSEL SOME MONTHS BACK.
HE WAS RESPONSIBLE FOR MY CAPTURE AND MY TIME IN PRISON!

MY CREW ATTACK'D HIS SHIP AT THE TIME, THE FUSELI. SINCE THEN I'VE BEEN PLOTTIN' MY REVENGE!
AYE, MY NEW CREW'LL WREAK 'AVOC A'EW ONC' WE M'TIN'R T'S V'S'L

DID YOU JUST... MAKE MORE RUM INSIDE YOUR BLOODSTREAM, BOSS?
AYE, I M'DE.
I M'DE.

I'M AFRAID THI'T E'EN ONE OF YOU IS ONE TOO MANY.
YOUR NUDITY SHOWS BRAVERY, BUT IT'S TIME YA WALKED THE METAPHORICAL SPACE-PLANK.

METAPHORICAL BECAUSE THEY DON'T MAKE THOSE ANYMORE.

NOW -- COMPUTER, PROCEED WITH ORIGINAL COURSE HEADING!
NOT SO FAST, PIRATE BREATH!

I ALWAYS WANTED TO SAY SOMETHING LIKE THUKKK

HE'S... ALIVE? ELSEWHERE?!
IS THIS THE WORK OF DRINK IN MY VEINS?
IS IT DRINK?!

CAPTAIN! WE'VE LOST HELM! AND SOMEONE'S ISSUING A DISTRESS BEACON!
ARRRIGHT! WE'VE GOT TO SPACE-HEAVE SPACE-HO!

BUT BLOW ALL THE AIRLOCKS ON THE WAY OUT. I DON'T WANT ANY OF THOSE QUADRUPLETS TO SURVIVE.

A2-Z! STILL NOT BACK UP YET. HOPEFULLY A TRANSPORT --
OH BOY -- URK --

MUST HAVE... BLOWN SOME OF THE AIRLOCKS AND DISABLED THE SAFETY FORCE WALLS!
HUKKRGLRK

HOPE I DON'T BURN THROUGH ALL MY CLONES BEFORE A2-Z CAN GET THIS UNDER CONTROL --
GGLBBKKK

THIS IS FASCINATING, BUT I'LL SEAL THE HULL NOW.

WE NARROWLY AVERTED OUR DEATHS IN COLD SPACE, BUT HOW MUCH LONGER WILL WE BE TRAPPED HERE?
WHAT IF SOMETHING WENT WRONG ON THE PARADIGM?

FALTON QUINE REPORTING FOR DUTY! ANYONE NEED A LIFT?

WHAT IN BLAZES TOOK YOU SO LONG? WERE YOU ASLEEP?

ARRR, YA DONE A MODERATELY REASONABLE JOB, RAMDEN.
THAT'S "EXCELLENT" ON THE PIRATE SCALE.
HERE'S WHAT I PROMISED.

IT'S TOUGH MAKING A NAME FOR YOURSELF AS THE SEXIEST, MOST SUAVE MERCENARY IN KNOWN SPACE.
MAYBE I'LL... WORK SOME OTHER SECTORS FOR A WHILE.
KINDA SCREWED THE GORGNATHIAN POOCH ON THIS ONE.
INFRA-REDBEARD
3333 AND 33/100
MERC WORK

WELL, THERE'S STILL PLENTY O' WORK IN THIS SECTOR IF YOU'RE GAME.
I WON'T SLEEP UNTIL I BEST THAT SPACE-CUR CUTTER EDGEWISE FOR ABANDONING THE PIRATE WAY.

THE GUY WITH THE EYEPATCH? I'D THINK YOU'D BE MORE UPSET AT THOSE QUINTUPLETS.
THEY WERE BRAVE. THEIR ONLY TRANSGRESS WAS MAKIN' ME SEE THEIR LOWSTUFF.

SEVERAL DAYS LATER.
CAPTAIN, WHY HAVE -- MAY I SPEAK CANDIDLY?
I'D PREFER YOU SPEAKING CANDIDLY TO SPEAKING CAN'T-DIDN'T-LY.

EVER SINCE I, WELL... RESCUED THE CREW AND THE PARADIGM FROM THE PIRATE HORDES, YOU'VE BEEN TALKING DOWN TO ME.
MR. QUINE, YOUR CLONES DID AN ADMIRABLE JOB OF DEFENDING THE SHIP.

MY UNDERSTANDING IS THOSE BRAVE QUINES GAVE THEIR LIVES IN SERVICE OF THIS VESSEL.
WHILE YOU JUST HELD YOUR BREATH UNTIL A2-Z RESTORED THE ATMOSPHERE.

IT DOESN'T SEEM... FAIR THE WAY THE CAPTAIN TREATS THE QUINE.
BECAUSE IT'S NOT ABOUT FAIRNESS. IT'S ABOUT EGO.

I'M THE ONE FILING THE OFFICIAL REPORT, AND VANDERBEAM WOULD DO WELL TO REMEMBER THAT.
IF HE THINKS HE CAN RUN THIS SHIP LIKE SOME PERSONAL SELF-CELEBRATION, HE'S WRONG!

I DON'T WANT PATS ON THE BACK.
I JUST WANT ACKNOWLEDGMENT FOR A JOB DONE BY THE BOOK.

AND PAPERWORK DONE BY SEVERAL HUNDRED BOOKS.

DID YOU GET THIS MEMO, CAPTAIN?
I GET ALL MEMOS, CUTTER. THE QUESTION IS, DO YOU?

WONDERFUL, I'LL ADD THAT ONE TO THE BALL.
I'M TALKING ABOUT THIS MEMO FROM STARCON'S HUMAN RESOURCES DEPARTMENT.

RUN THE GIST BY ME -- I HAVE TO MANAGE THE STARS.
"THE BRIDGE CREW OF THE PARADIGM HAS BEEN ORDERED TO PARTICIPATE IN SENSITIVITY TRAINING."

ONE WORD OR LESS, PLEASE. VERY BUSY.

WHY SHOULD I HAVE TO ATTEND SENSITIVITY TRAINING?!
WHAT CAPTAIN CRIES MORE AT THE BEAUTY OF THESE SAARINEN-INSPIRED CEILINGS?!

THIS COMES STRAIGHT FROM THE TOP BRASS. WELL, NOT THE TOP BRASS BECAUSE THEY GOT BETTER THINGS TO DO.

I'M CRYING RIGHT NOW! OH, IDLE TEARS! I KNOW NOT WHAT THEY MEAN!
MAYBE THAT'S NOT A POSITIVE.

ANNOUNCEMENT: I WILL NOT BE ATTENDING SENSITIVITY TRAINING DUE TO OVERSENSITIVITY.

DO I HAVE TO ATTEND THE SENSITIVITY CLASS, SIR?
IT'S THE ENTIRE BRIDGE CREW, SO PROBABLY.

EXCUSE ME, SIR, BUT IN A PREVIOUS EVALUATION I WAS TOLD "MR. JINX'S SPINELESS OVER-SENSITIVITY BORDERS ON LIABILITY."
I REMEMBER WHEN I SAID THAT, YES.

BUT A LOT'S CHANGED, JINX. MAYBE YOU'VE TOUGHENED UP SINCE THEN.
MAYBE YOU'VE GOTTEN SO TOUGH THAT YOU JUST NEED A REFRESHER.

OH NO, I'M TOO TOUGH.

MR. JINX! DID YOU ORGANIZE THIS TRAINING CLASS?
NO, SIR. I THOUGHT PERHAPS YOU HAD.
NO! WHO FELT THIS WAS NEEDED?

HOLIDAY! DID YOU HAVE CONCERNS OF SENSITIVITY?
ME?

WHAT VEIN OF SENSITIVITIES HAS BEEN REFUSED YOUR PERSON THAT I CAN DELIVER UNTO YOU?
ARE YOU SENSITIVE RIGHT NOW?
I'M DESPERATE TO EXPOSE THAT QUIVERING BED OF NERVE!

YOU'RE REFERRING TO THE CLASS? RIGHT? ... RIGHT?
BLAST IT, MERIDIAN! I WILL HAVE A CAPTAIN'S SATISFACTION!

ALL RIGHT, GENTLEHUMANS -- MY NAME IS PROFESSOR TEUTHIS, AND TODAY WE'RE GOING TO TALK ABOUT "SENSITIVITY IN THE WORKPLACE."
"INTERCESSOR-CLASS STAR CRUISER EDITION."

QUESTION: SHOULD WE RANK THE MOST SENSITIVE AMONG US AND NOT MAKE THEM WASTE THEIR TIME WITH THIS?
MR. JINX AND I ARE SOFT TO THE TOUCH.

WHAT ABOUT ME? I HAVE A LOT TO GET DONE.
YES, HOLIDAY HAS A CERTAIN FEMININE CHARM.

CUTTER HAS TO STAY. HE'S ABOUT AS SENSITIVE AS A KILRATHI TOILET SEAT.
I WISH HE WAS WRONG.

SO, PROF, I GUESS YOU GOT BUSTED DOWN FROM TEACHING AT THE ACADEMY TO DAYCARE.
HAVE WE MET? I'VE ONLY READ YOUR FILE, MR. EDGEWISE.

AS HAVE WE ALL! CAPTAIN MEMNON VANDERBEAM HERE, SENSITIVE AND ACADEMY-TESTED.
IT SEEMS I ALREADY CONTAIN ALL YOU CAN IMPART.

I'M SORRY, CAPTAIN, BUT THE BRIDGE CREW MUST TAKE THE COURSE. EVERYONE EXCEPT A MR. QUINE, AND A MS. RAQUEL.

SO ANYONE WITH A Q IN THEIR NAME? MY MIDDLE NAME IS... QU... QUIET.
IT'S AN OLD EARTH NAME.
REALLY.

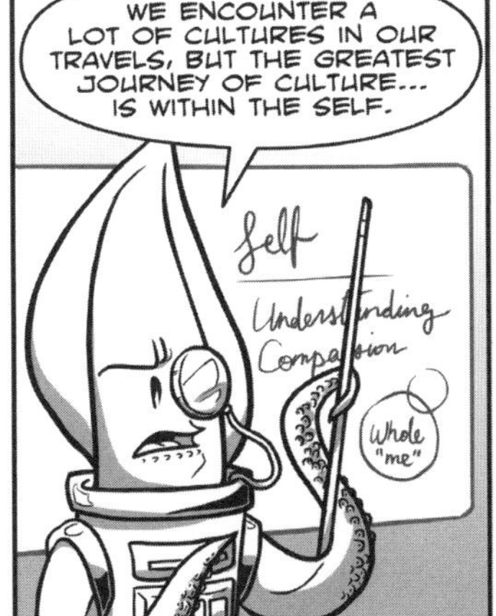
WE ENCOUNTER A LOT OF CULTURES IN OUR TRAVELS, BUT THE GREATEST JOURNEY OF CULTURE... IS WITHIN THE SELF.
Self
Understanding
Compassion
Whole "me"

THIS IS HOW YOU BEGIN YOUR LECTURE? ON CULTURE? DO YOU REALIZE WHO YOU'RE SPEAKING WITH?!

I WAS CURATOR OF THE FUSELI FOR A DECADE!!
I'M THE MOST SENSITIVE PERSON IN THE GALAXY.

WHAT WOULD YOU DO, THEN, IF A YOUNG PARINESH FEMALE ASKED
CARESS HER OUTERMOST CLAW PAIR.

WHAT I WANNA KNOW IS WHY QUINE AND RAQUEL ARE EXEMPT FROM THIS THING.
QUINE LIKELY KNOWS THESE RULES BACKWARDS AND FORWARDS, SIR.
Love
Hate
Feelings

I'M PRETTY SURE IT'S MORE THAN THAT.
QUINE PROBABLY DOESN'T LIKE HOW HE'S BEEN TREATED LATELY, SIR.

HE SAVED THE SHIP AT GREAT INJURY TO HIMSELF AND GOT NO CREDIT.
RAQUEL IS ABOUT THE ONLY SYMPATHETIC CREW MEMBER TO HIM, SO HE FELT SHE DIDN'T NEED THE COURSE.

NO, I'M PRETTY SURE IT'S BECAUSE QUINE IS A PENCIL-PUSHING JERK. WE'LL GET HIM GOOD.
SHENANIGANS ON QUINE! GENTS, I'M IN.

EMPATHY IS PARAMOUNT. TO PUT YOURSELF IN THE PLACE OF ANOTHER.
CAPTAIN, IS THAT A SKILL YOU POSSESS?
OUT. RAGE. OUS.

I CAN **EVEN** IMAGINE BEING THAT BUREAUCRAT **QUINE!**
UNABLE TO **EXPRESS** YOURSELF OUTSIDE OF PROTOCOLS, RULES. HAVING LOST TOUCH WITH YOUR OWN HUMANITY.
PERHAPS WANTING TO. PERHAPS **HOPING** OTHERS WILL UNDERSTAND.

ONE'S SENSE OF BELONGING, THAT WE **ALL** HAVE A RIGHT TO, SNUFFED OUT BY **DUTY.**
A SILENT BURDEN, A BEAUTIFUL VISE ON THE HEART. LIKE A GILDED PENDULUM.
LIKE **TIME.** TIME, OUR **BETRAYER.**

OH QUINE, I AM SORRY.

ARE YOU GOING TO TELL QUINE YOU'RE SORRY FOR MISTREATING HIM?
NO, NO. I FEAR IT WOULD BE TOO LITTLE, TOO LATE.

BUT I **CAN ENDEAVOUR** TO CHANGE MY **BEHAVIOUR** IN THE **FUTOURE.**
I HAVE DENIED HIM THE MILK OF HUMAN KINDNESS. NOW, I INVITE HIM TO **NURSE.**

ARE YOU GOING TO TELL QUINE YOU
BECAUSE OF A CLASS? GIVE ME. A. BREAK.
QUINE IS **DOOMED.**

MR. QUINE! A WORD!
HERE WE GO.

I JUST WANTED TO SAY FORCING US TO TAKE THAT COURSE WAS VERY INFORMATIVE.
I APPRECIATE ALL THAT YOU DO.

WELL... THANK YOU FOR APPROACHING IT WITH AN OPEN MIND!
I MEAN, THE RESPONSE I EXPECTED TO GET

How the Jinxlets Saved *the* SPACE ZOO

An Activity Coloring Pad for Children Ages 3 and Up

Non-Terran Species: Use Included Worksheet To Determine Equivalent Age

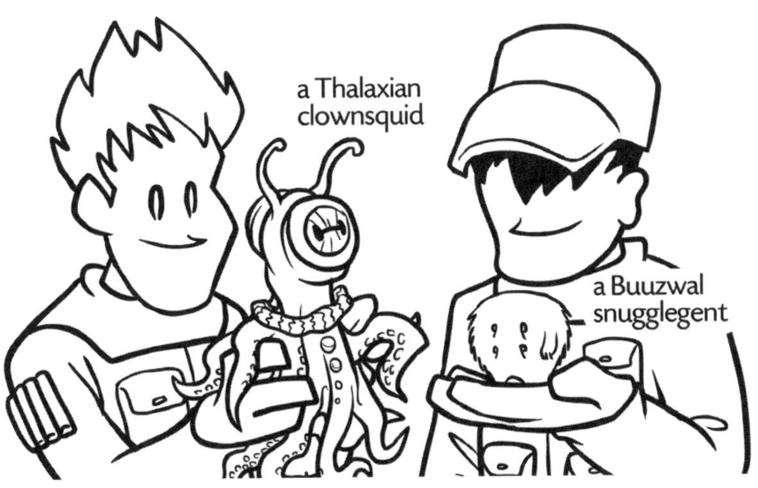

Chiff and Ayler were two zookeepers. They worked at the space zoo, near a very big planet.

It was a very big space zoo with all kinds of animals from all around the universe.

What is your favorite animal?

Note To Parents: Use Attached Psychological Profile Sheet To Determine If Child's Favorite Animal Denotes Psychotic Or Antisocial Tendencies

Jinxlets are blue and round and fuzzy. They have two big eyes and two floppy ears.

Jinxlets were new to the space zoo. There were so many Jinxlets! No one knew quite what to do with them all.

If Child Indicates That Destroying An Overpopulous Species Within A Controlled Habitat Is A Valid Course Of Action, Refer To Behavioral Flowchart D

One day, Chiff and Ayler noticed something wrong with the other animals in the space zoo. They seemed to be scared of something. They weren't even eating their food!

What was going on? How could they help?

Note: Teach Children Not All Foods Are Equivalent In Terms Of Xenobiological Pet Sustenance

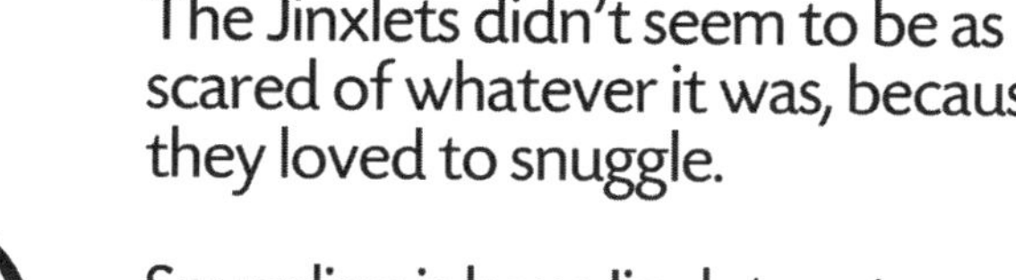

The Jinxlets didn't seem to be as scared of whatever it was, because they loved to snuggle.

Snuggling is how Jinxlets eat and play.

Caution: Inform Your Child Of The Dangers Of Proximal Metacaloric Energy Transfer When Involved With Animal Life Other Than That Described Within United Star Configuration Class H Xenobiological Parameters

Minors Can Apply For A Personal LEXR-NEXR Study License To Peruse The Xenobiology Rules And Regulations Database With Provided Guardian Consent

Snuggling May Not Be Adequate Feeding For Other Types Of Pets; Consult SCXP Guidelines Before Proceeding With A Given Snuggle Regimen

Chiff said, "I have a great idea!"

"What is it?" asked Ayler.

"We could let the Jinxlets snuggle the other animals. Maybe then they wouldn't be so scared, and they'd eat their food again."

Do Not Allow A Pet To Engage In Unsupervised Contact With Another Species

Chiff and Ayler put Jinxlets into each animal's cage.

Chiff was right! The Jinxlets calmed the other creatures down enough so they could eat their dinners.

But why had the animals been so scared?

Also Available: *I Have Two Jinxlets, A Jinxlet Kwanzaa, Dirk Snugbirk, Jinxlet P.I. - For Young Adults*

Suddenly two people appeared. Chiff and Ayler didn't know who they were.

"Don't be afraid," said the man.

The woman said, "my name is Xxxyyy and this is my friend, The Chronomantic."

Warning: Let Your Children Know About Temporal Stranger Danger

* IN THE CRISIS STORYLINE "FUTURE WAR"

* THE PARTICLES INSIDE QUARKS.

"Thanks, little Jinxlet, for all your help calming down the animals," said the friendly old man.

"Now we'll use our special powers to save the zoo!"

The Thurabsh Red-Threaded Skyosk Is Not Likely To Wing Over A Celebration In A Friendly Manner; It Is Responsible For Hundreds Of Thurab Injuries

Thurabsh red-threaded skyosk

So the Space Zoo was saved, thanks to the zookeepers who paid good attention, and the visitors who wanted to help out, and of course, the Jinxlets -- because caring about others is what they do best!

All Venge Kingthrawls Were Presumed Extinct At Press Time

my house

WERE THESE PEOPLE REAL, PROCTOR?
YES, MAVERICK. THEY ALL LIVED LONG, LONG AGO, IN THE PAST.

THEY WERE TIME CRIMINALS.
AND WHEN YOU GET OLDER, YOU'LL GO BACK THERE AND KILL THEM.

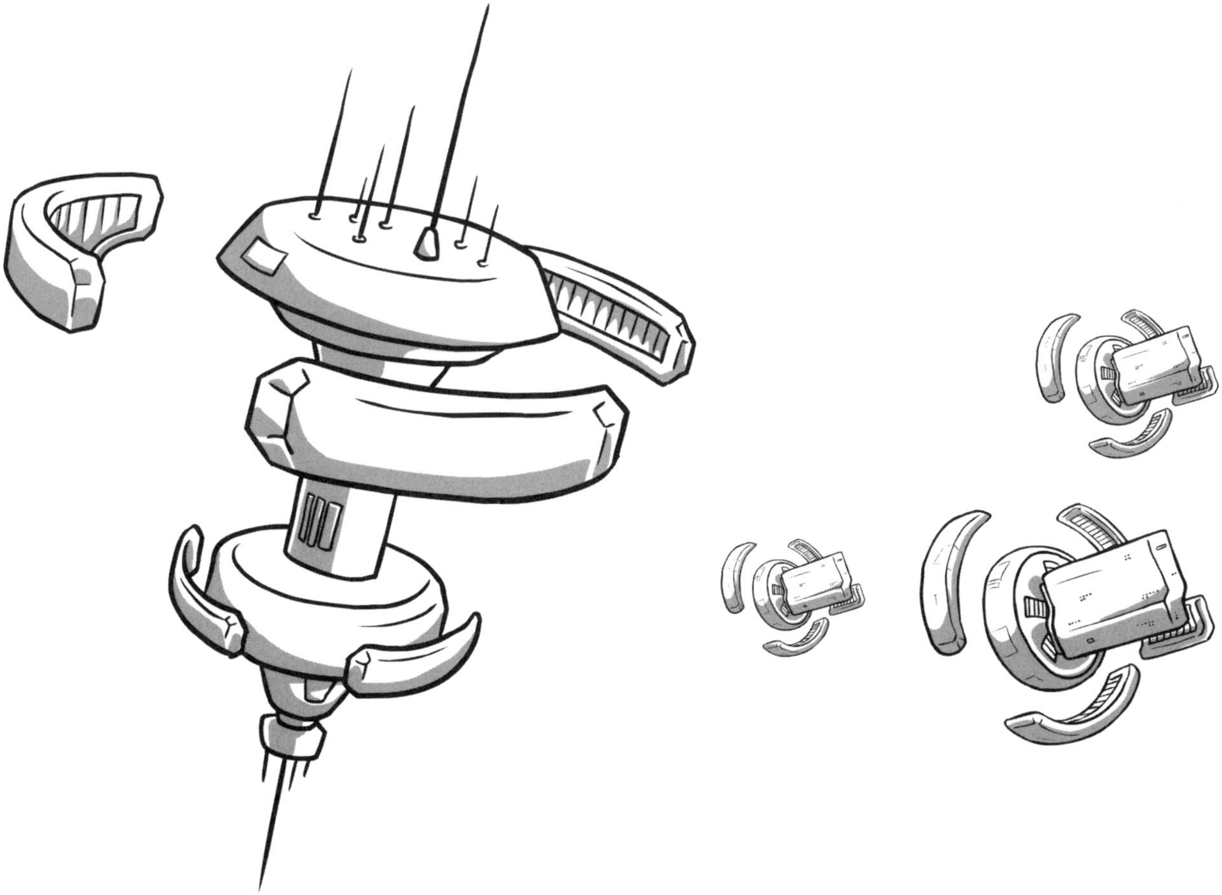

NEW ORDERS HAVE ARRIVED FROM ADMIRAL HUFF, SIR.
ORDERS, ORDERS, ORDERS! IT'S SO... MILITARISTIC.

CAN'T WE DO BETTER THAN ONE ENTITY ORDERING ANOTHER AROUND?
PERHAPS IF THERE WAS A REVIEW PROCESS OR INITIAL RIGHT OF REFUSAL ONE COULD GIVE.
IT'S AS IF MY THOUGHTS DON'T MATTER AT ALL!

LET US TRY THIS. REGARDLESS OF WHAT THE ORDER IS, INFORM HUFF THAT I WISH TO DISCUSS IT WITH HIM.
HE MAY PERCEIVE THIS WILLINGNESS TO COLLABORATE AS A POSITIVE!

IN THAT CASE, I HAVE A SUGGESTION, SIR --
BLEAH. THE SYSTEM WORKS. JUST READ IT TO ME.

THE PARADIGM IS ORDERED TO RETURN TO QUELLAR?!
THAT DELIGHTFULLY CHALLENGED WORLD IN THE NEBULA?!

WE'RE SUPPOSED TO CHECK UP ON THE PROGRESS OF THEIR CIVILIZATION.
AFTER WE WRECKED THEIR HIVE MIND.
GENTLY PUSHING A STALLED VEHICLE ISN'T "WRECKING."

BESIDES, WHY THEY WOULD SEND US? ASIDE FROM THAT LITTLE OOPS, WE HAVE NO CONNECTION WITH THE QUEL!

WE HAVE A QUEL CREWMEMBER!
BUT IS SHE STILL CONSIDERED A QUEL? WE WRECKED THEIR HIVE MIND.

STARCON IS ENTERING INTO A TECHNOLOGY EXCHANGE PROGRAM WITH THE QUEL.
IT'S SORT OF OUR APOLOGY.

THEY'RE GIVING US MEDICAL EQUIPMENT. SOME OF THEIR APPROACHES TO HEALING ARE FASCINATING.
WHEN YOU DON'T FEAR DEATH, YOU LEARN A LOT ABOUT THE BODY'S TOLERANCES.

IN EXCHANGE WE'RE GIVING THEM THIS NANOTECH SUITE.
IT'LL HELP THEM GET MORE USED TO LIVING WITHOUT A HIVE MIND.

NANOBOTS? WHAT DO THEY DO?
LIVE IN THEIR EARS AND WHISPER "THERE, THERE" MOSTLY.

THE NANOTECH WILL BE IN THE VAULT IN MY INFIRMARY.
CUTTER, SINCE YOU'RE SECURITY LEAD, I'LL NEED GUARDS POSTED.
INFIRMARY

ALSO THAT INFORMATION IS CONFIDENTIAL. STRICTLY NEED-TO-KNOW BASIS.
MARY

THANKS, CHIEF!

I HATE DAHK'S VOICE. SOUNDS LIKE SOMEONE BLOWING INTO PUDDING WITH A STRAW.

ONE WEEK LATER
NEXT STOP QUELLAR! WE'LL TAKE A RELEVATOR TO THE SURFACE AND MEET WITH THEIR COUNCIL IN 36 HOURS.
DAHK, BE A DEAR AND PREPARE OUR NANOTECH HOUSEWARMING GIFT.

YES, CAPTAIN! QUITE A MARVEL THESE NANOBOTS.
THEY WILL ACT AS A TEMPORARY SALVE FOR THESE POOR QUEL'S PSIONIC ORGANS.

WONDERFUL! HERE'S TO A FRESH, TROUBLE-FREE REBOOT TO OUR RELATIONSHIP!
TO OUR UPCOMING SHARED NEW ERA!!
MUCH LIKE A NEW YEAR'S CELEBRATION!

CAPTAIN! THE NANO CYLINDER -- IT'S GONE! IT'S BEEN STOLEN!!
SOUNDS LIKE THIS YEAR'S BALL... JUST DROPPED.

HOW COULD ANYONE GET PAST THE GUARDS? HAVE THE KEYCARD TO THIS VAULT?
THERE ISN'T EVEN EVIDENCE THAT ANYTHING WAS HACKED OR BROKEN INTO!

HMM. HMM.

I THINK THIS CALLS FOR A LITTLE OLD-FASHIONED DETECTIVE WORK.
SADDLE UP, JINX -- WE GOT A CRIME TO SOLVE.

EXCEPT THAT LITERALLY EVERYTHING ON THIS SHIP IS RECORDED AT ALL TIMES AND WE'LL HAVE THE ANSWER IN JUST SECONDS.
WELL, HELL.

YOU KNOW WHO USED TO PUT A LOT OF STOCK IN DETECTIVE WORK?
PROBABLY PIRATES, SIR.
THE PIRATES DID.

WHEN YOU'VE GOT A THIEF ON BOARD A THREE-HUNDRED-YEAR-OLD SHIP WITHOUT ALL THIS RECON TECHNOLOGY, YOU NEED A GOOD DICK ON YOUR SIDE.
NOWADAYS, YOU CAN GET A GUY'S DNA FROM ENHANCING HIS PICTURE.

ANYWAY, A2-Z -- WHAT DO THE LOGS SHOW?
LET'S SEE... HUH. IT APPEARS AS THOUGH THOSE SECTORS OF MY MEMORY WERE DELETED.

CUTTER EDGEWISE INTERSTELLAR P.I.

THE INFIRMARY IS SPOTLESS, SIR. WHOEVER STOLE THE NANOTECH KNEW HOW TO COVER THEIR TRACKS.
THAT LEAVES OUT DAHK. HE'S SLIMING UP THE WHOLE PLACE.

IT LOOKS LIKE ALL CREW POSITION LOGS WERE WIPED FOR THE ENTIRE DECK.
NO EVIDENCE. THAT LEAVES MOTIVE.

SALES OF BLACK MARKET NANOTECH MENTAL ENHANCEMENTS HAVE INCREASED IN RECENT MONTHS, SIR.
GOOD THOUGHT -- BUT WE'RE TOO FAR AWAY FOR THAT TO BE WORTHWHILE.

PEOPLE WHO USE MACHINES TO ALTER THEIR BRAIN CHEMISTRY DISGUST ME.

ALL RIGHT, RAQUEL. I THOUGHT WE WERE PALS. I SHOWED YOU THE MAGIC OF DRINKING.
BUT WHY WOULD I STEAL THE STARCON'S NANOTECH?

YOU'RE THE ONE CLOSEST TO THE QUEL! THE NANOTECH WAS FOR ALL YOUR PEOPLE!
MAYBE YOU'VE SIDED WITH ONE OF THE NEW FACTIONS AND WANT THEM TO HAVE THE ADVANTAGE!
UNLESS YOU GOT A WITNESS TO YOUR WHEREABOUTS, YOU'RE UP SWAMBLE CREEK!!

I HAVE... A WITNESS... WHO CAN. ATTEST TO. MY WHEREABOUTS.
OH YEAH?

... AUGH. AUGH! YOU GUYS. YOU GUYS ARE GROSS.

WELL, SCRATCH THOSE CRAZY KIDS RAQUEL AND QUINE. HOW CAN WE HAVE NO MOTIVE AT ALL?
WITHOUT MOTIVE WE MUST RETURN TO EVIDENCE, SIR.

AND WITHOUT EVIDENCE, WE MUST TURN TO *LACK* OF EVIDENCE.
THERE IS ONLY *ONE* PERSON ON THIS SHIP WHO KNOWS HOW TO MANIPULATE A COMPUTER INTERFACE LIKE ME.

HEAD ENGINEER MERIDIAN LEE HOLIDAY.

... HMMF?

BUT WHY WOULD *I* STEAL NANOTECHNOLOGY?!
HOLIDAY, LOOK AT THE FACTS FOR YOURSELF. HOW SHOULD I MOVE FORWARD?

ALL THE LOGS HAVE BEEN WIPED. TELEM SHOWS NO TIME TRAVEL ACTIVITY. THE TWO GUARDS ARE BOY SCOUTS IN *PERFECT* STANDING AND DIDN'T SEE A THING.
THE ONLY CLUE WE HAVE THAT EVEN PINS DOWN A *TIMEFRAME* IS THE DELETED LOGS.
YOU'RE THE *ONLY PERSON* WHO KNOWS HOW TO DO THAT.

YOU DON'T *SEEM* TO HAVE A MOTIVE. BUT MAYBE YOU'RE BEING BLACKMAILED OR COERCED.
YOU'RE GONNA HAVE TO COME WITH ME.

YOU'RE THROWING ME IN THE BRIG??
YEAH, BUT WE'LL GET A DRINK FIRST.

THIS IS THE KIND OF QUICK ACTION STARCON NEEDED TO ASSUAGE THE QUEL, CUTTER.
I HADN'T EXPECTED THE INCARCERATION OF OUR *LEAD ENGINEER*.
ME NEITHER.

I KNOW THE BRASS HAVE BEEN PUSHING FOR A BREAK IN THIS THING, SO I GAVE THEM ONE. BUT IT'LL FALL APART SOON.
THE ONLY THINGS HOLIDAY'S *GUILTY* OF ARE BEING AN AMAZING SPORT AND EATING AT HER WORK CONSOLE.
C R M

WHAT'S NEXT?
TALK IT THROUGH WITH THE PRINCIPALS. THE TWO GUARDS. DAHK. ANYONE ANYWHERE NEAR THE SCENE AT THE TIME IN QUESTION.

ALSO, DON'T THINK I HAVEN'T NOTICED THE HAT. *VERY* TASK-APPROPRIATE.
IN HIS ERA, ZAC EFRON WAS CONSIDERED A *MASTER* DETECTIVE.
FILE IMAGE

I CAN'T PERCEIVE ANY ABNORMALITIES IN THE VAULT LOCKING MECHANISM.
SPECTROGRAPHIC ANALYSIS DIDN'T EVEN SHOW ELEVATED TEMPERATURES IN HERE FOLLOWING THE THEFT.
I CHECKED DOWN TO THE LEVEL OF ATOMIC MOTION.

WHOEVER IT WAS KNEW HOW TO LAND A PUNCH, AND USE A VOCODER TO SPEAK THROUGH.
THIS IS WHAT THE PLAN IS, EDGEWISE.

THE NANOTECH IS GONE. THE TALKS END NOW. THE ASTRY AND THE QUELLAR GO SEPARATE WAYS.
THE INTERFERENCE STOPS HERE.

I REMEMBERED MY "STAB HILTWARD: PIRATE DETECTIVE" BOOKS. MAYBE IF I GOADED THIS GUY SOME MORE HE'D MAKE A MISTAKE.
WHERE'D YOU LEARN TO PUNCH LIKE THAT, IN BETWEEN DOILY-KNITTING AND TEACUP-POLISHING AT GIRL SCHOOL?

JUDGING FROM THE RESPONSE, THE GUY HAD SOME AMAZING-LOOKING TEA CUPS.

SIR, ARE YOU ALL RIGHT? YOU LOOK EVEN WORSE THAN USUAL.
I SAW A MAN ABOUT A MEAT TENDERIZER LAST NIGHT.

WE SHOULD PULL THE LOGS BEFORE THEY GET ERASED AGAIN, SIR.
I GUARANTEE THEY'VE ALREADY BEEN. AND IT WASN'T HOLIDAY, WHICH WE KNEW.
BUT THAT DOESN'T MATTER ANYWAY.

HAVE VANDERBEAM ROUND EVERYONE UP IN THE INFIRMARY. TURNS OUT I DON'T NEED COMPUTER LOGS TO KNOW WHO DID IT.
IT'S WHO DUN IT, SIR.
WHO SAYS?
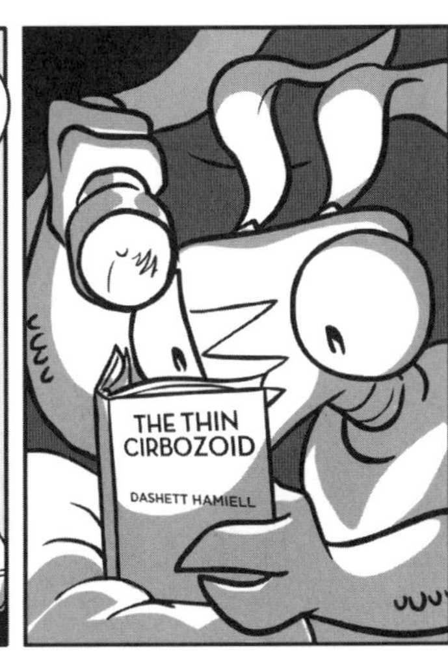
THE THIN CIRBOZOID
DASHETT HAMIELL

CUTTER, WHAT'S THE MEANING OF THIS THEATRICALITY?!
YOU KNOW I DON'T ROUSE UNTIL 0745. I'M STILL IN WAKING-SNUGGLE PHASE!!
DO THE REST OF YOUR SNUGGLING SITTING UP, CAPTAIN.

THE NANOTECH THIEF IS IN THIS ROOM. AND I'M GOING TO EXPLAIN HOW I KNOW.
AH! A TRADITIONAL DETECTIVE TROPE TO TANTALIZE THE SENSES! HOW THRILLING.

EVEN THOUGH DAHK WAS THE LAST GUY TO SEE THE TUBE, I DON'T SUSPECT HIM.
HE'S A LITTLE SCATTERBRAINED. ESPECIALLY SINCE HIS BRAIN CAN LITERALLY SCATTER INSIDE HIS BODY.

AND I DON'T SUSPECT CREWMAN KLEPTOR FROM THE PILFERTRON SYSTEM BECAUSE HE JUST TRANSFERRED IN THIS MORNING. YOU CAN LEAVE.
WHEW.

I THOUGHT HOLIDAY WAS THE ONLY EXPERT-LEVEL TECH ON THE SHIP. BUT I WAS **WRONG.**
THE PROBLEM IS, KNOWING YOUR WAY AROUND AN **A.I.** LIKE A2-Z IS ONLY HALF THE JOB...
... ON A DECK FULL OF POTENTIAL **WITNESSES,** WITH TWO GUARDS POSTED.

SOMEONE WOULD HAVE TO KNOW HOW TO HACK A MIND AS WELL AS AN INTERFACE.
TRIGGERING THE VAULT DOOR IS CHILD'S PLAY COMPARED TO WIPING A **MEMORY.**

QUINE. THE FIRST TIME WE MET RAQUEL, DIDN'T SHE **BLANK YOU OUT** FOR A LONG PERIOD?
YES. I HAD NO MEMORY OF HOW I'D GOTTEN THERE!

BUT I DID NOT **DO** THIS, THE CUTTER!
NO, YOU DIDN'T. BECAUSE WE HAVE **ANOTHER QUEL ON BOARD.**

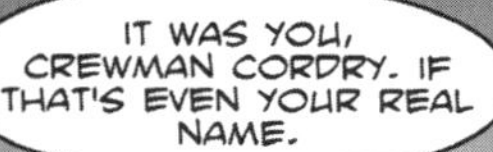

IT WAS YOU, CREWMAN CORDRY. IF THAT'S EVEN YOUR REAL NAME.
IF I WERE OF THE QUEL, WOULDN'T I HAVE A PSIONIC ORGAN? AND BE **BALD?**

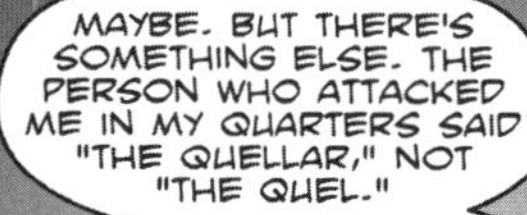

MAYBE. BUT THERE'S SOMETHING ELSE. THE PERSON WHO ATTACKED ME IN MY QUARTERS SAID "THE QUELLAR," NOT "THE QUEL."
QUEL HAVE A PROBLEM WITH ARTICLES. THEY DON'T THINK OF THEIR PLANET AND THEIR SPECIES AS SEPARATE.
I KNEW I WAS ATTACKED BY A **QUEL.**

THAT BRINGS US TO YOU, CORDRY. YOU GET HUNG UP ON THE WORD **"THE"** TOO.
OH, IT'S **TECHNICALLY** GOOD ENGLISH. BUT YOU ALWAYS GO THE LONG WAY TO SAY IT. EVERY TIME.
"OF THE QUEL?" WHY NOT "IF I WERE QUEL?" BECAUSE YOU'RE NOT SURE IF THAT'S **CORRECT.**

THE DETECTIVE IS A LITTLE TOO CLEVER FOR HIS OWN GOOD.

YOU'RE OF THE QUEL, BUT... **SUNDERER!!**
YES. I **AM** OF THE SUNDERER CELL.

THOUGH THE QUEL **DESPISES** THE THOUGHT OF LEAVING ITS PERFECT WORLD IN THE NEBULA, THERE WERE THOSE OF US BORN WITH **WEAKER** PSIONIC ORGANS.
WE BELIEVED THE QUEL SHOULD EXPAND INTO THE UNIVERSE, TO SEEK, TO **LEARN.** THEY DISAGREED.

OUR GOAL HAS ALWAYS BEEN THE DESTRUCTION OF THE HIVE MIND.
THE A.I. WAS **SIMPLE** TO CIRCUMVENT. INFLUENCING THE GUARDS AND THE DOCTOR WERE EVEN **SIMPLER.**

BUT WHERE'S YOUR HEAD ANTENNA? AND YOUR BALDNESS?
ON THE INSIDE. AND **THIS IS A WIG.**

HAND OVER THE TUBE, SUNDERER. THIS MESS CAN ALL BE UNDONE.
THE TUBE IS THE **CAUSE** OF THE MESS IN THE FIRST PLACE!

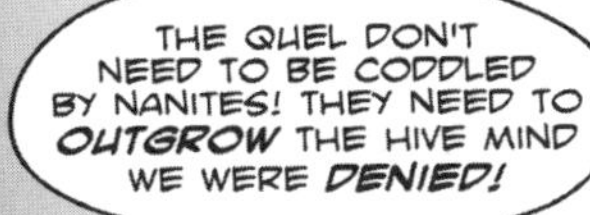
THE QUEL DON'T NEED TO BE CODDLED BY NANITES! THEY NEED TO **OUTGROW** THE HIVE MIND WE WERE **DENIED!**

WE WERE THE SUBCASTE ON QUELLAR! NOW THE QUEL MUST CHANGE TO **OUR** WAY OR **DIE!!**

IT'S NOT YOUR DECISION TO MAKE! HAND OVER THE TUBE.
YOU CAN HAVE THE TUBE OVER YOUR OWN **DEAD BODY.**

WHUPK
YOW WOW WOW
OKAY YES YOU CAN HAVE THE TUBE YOU CAN HAVE THE TUBE

GOOD **SPACE** HEAVENS, CUTTER! YOU SOLVED THE CASE USING ONLY YOUR **HOOCH-SOAKED CEREBRUM!**
I GOT HIT IN THE FACE A COUPLE TIMES TOO, SO. THAT COUNTS.

THE NANOTECH IS IN MY QUARTERS. I CHANGED THE INTERNAL TELEM ARRAY SO YOU COULDN'T DETECT IT.
BUT HOW DID YOU AVOID BEING FOUND OUT DURING YOUR STARCON PHYSICALS?

I JUST CLOUDED THE MIND OF THE PHYSICIAN, THEN HACKED THE MEDICON.
THAT DOESN'T EXPLAIN WHY ANY OF THE BIOMETRICS ON THE SHIP WORK WITH YOUR BODY.

I HAD TO ADAPT CUTANEOUS DNA STRANDS TO FIT --
AUGH! CASE CLOSED! I'M TELLING THE ADMIRAL I DID EVERYTHING.

CAPTAIN'S BLOG, SPACE-TIME RIGHT NOW.
WITH THE RECOVERY OF THE NANOTECHNOLOGY, TALKS WITH THE QUEL HAVE **REOPENED.**
STARCON, HOWEVER, IS INTERESTED IN MAKING SURE THERE ARE NO **HARD FEELINGS.**
RAQUEL, WE WANTED TO MAKE SURE YOUR PEOPLE STILL FEEL **GOOD** ABOUT ACCEPTING THIS EXCHANGE.
I THINK THE QUEL JUST WANT THEIR HIVE MIND, OR SOMETHING LIKE IT, TO COME BACK.
THE CUTTER HAS BEEN EXTREMELY HELPFUL. HE IS A HERO TO MY PEOPLE.

A2-Z, MAKE SURE THAT'S ALL INCLUDED IN THE REPORT. EXCEPT FOR THAT MAUDLIN ADDENDUM.
I'M REPORTING IT VERBATIM.
PUT THAT I SAID THAT PART, THEN.

MY FRIENDS WONDER WHY I CALL YOU ALL THE TIME, WHAT CAN I SAY
I DON'T FEEL THE NEED TO GIVE SUCH SECRETS AWAY

YOU THINK MAYBE I NEED HELP, NO, I KNOW THAT I'M RIGHT
I'M JUST BETTER OFF NOT LISTENING TO FRIENDS' ADVICE

WHEN THEY INSIST ON KNOWING MY BLISS I TELL THEM THIS
WHEN THEY WANT TO KNOW WHAT THE REASON IS
I ONLY SMILE WHEN I LIE, THEN I TELL THEM WHY

BOTH OF YOU HAVE TO FILE PAPERWORK TO REGISTER AS A COUPLE IMMEDIATELY OR I WILL LOSE MY JOB.

ADMIRAL HUFF ON COMMUNIQUE FOR YOU, CAPTAIN.
NO DOUBT WITH CONGRATULATIONS FOR THE CREW! LET'S HAVE HIM ON SHIPWIDE.

VANDERBEAM. LET EDGEWISE KNOW HE HANDLED THIS THE BEST WAY POSSIBLE. GOOD WORK.
GOOD WORK, TO BOTH OF US. NOTED AND LOGGED.

SIGH. YES, I SAID SIGH.
WE'RE RECALLING THE PARADIGM AND A TON OF OTHER ACTIVE VESSELS BACK TO THE SOL SYSTEM.

TRY TO MANAGE THAT WITHOUT CREATING AN INTERSTELLAR INCIDENT.
YOUR CONFIDENCE IS ALL THE REASSURANCE I NEED TO COMPLETE THIS UNDERTAKING, YOUR ADMIRALTY.
NU

CUTTER, WHY WOULD THE FLEET AMASS AT EARTH?
ONE OF TWO THINGS.

EITHER WE'RE BEING ORDERED TO ATTACK LOS ANGELES, OR STARCON IS HOLDING A ROUND OF MOCK FLEET BATTLES.
AH YES, WE'VE BEEN TO THOSE BEFORE!

WE HAVE BEEN TO THEM. WHAT WE HAVEN'T DONE IS COME ANYWHERE NEAR WINNING THEM.
THE PARADIGM IS ONE OF THE FLEET'S BIGGEST STAR CRUISERS. WE SHOULD BE AT THE TOP OF THAT LIST!

I KNOW YOU'RE STILL UPSET ABOUT ALL THE TIMES WE FORGOT TO OPEN FIRE.
I ALWAYS JUST... GET CAUGHT UP IN THE PAGEANTRY.

CONSIDERABLY LATER, NEAR EARTH
LOOK AT ALL THESE SHIPS! THERE HAVEN'T BEEN THIS MANY IN ONE PLACE SINCE THE ACTION OVER CIRBOZOID.

WOW! THERE'S THE SMALLER SISTER OF THE FUSELI, THE SUMMER RHYME.
I FIGURED SHE'D BE OUT OF SERVICE BY NOW.

YIKES. WHAT IS THAT MONSTROSITY?
THAT'S THE EXEMPLAR. HER FIRST COMMISSION WAS UNDER VARIUS TRASK, THE ASTRY'S MOST FAMED CAPTAIN.

HER JUTTING BOSOM COULD TOPPLE THE HEAVENS.
I'LL SAY. UNDER VARIOUS CIRCUMSTANCES.

THIS IS ADMIRAL HUFF SPEAKING TO THE ASSEMBLED FLEET.
WELCOME TO OUR ANNUAL MOCK FLEET BATTLE TRAINING EXERCISES.

RIGHT NOW YOUR SCIENCE OFFICER IS RECEIVING DATA ON FLEET ORGANIZATION.
YOU WILL EACH BE ASSIGNED TO A TACTICAL GROUP, AND WILL BE PERFORMING A SERIES OF FIELD TESTS.

THIS WEEK WILL END WITH THE TRADITIONAL ALL-OUT BATTLE FOR THE TITLE OF ASTRY FLEETSPERSON.
OF COURSE, LAST YEAR'S WIN WENT TO THE CAPTAIN OF THE EXEMPLAR,

THERIN ZARDE.
EVERY YEAR, USING A SOPHISTICATED ALGORITHM, I PICK A SHIP TO HATE.

ZARDE! THE JERK I BESTED AT THE ACADEMY IN THAT ALTERNATE UNIVERSE.
BUT IN THIS UNIVERSE, I NEVER ATTENDED, SO ZARDE PROBABLY GOT HIS PICK OF CRUISERS.

HE REALLY HAD IT IN FOR YOU, CUTTER.
LUCKILY, IN THIS UNIVERSE, YOU NEVER MET AND HE HAS NO IDEA WHO ANY OF US ARE.

PARADIGM, EH? CAPTAIN VANDERBEAM? THIS IS CAPTAIN ZARDE. YOU LOOK LIKE A REAL CHUMP.
I DON'T KNOW WHAT IT IS ABOUT YOUR SHIP, BUT I CAN'T STAND THE SHAPE OF IT. OH YEAH. YOU'RE GOING DOWN.

WHO'S THAT THERE? YOUR SECURITY POST? ONE-EYE? FORGET YOU, VANDERBEAM, THAT'S A GUY I COULD LEARN TO HATE.
I ALREADY HATE HIM SO MUCH I'M GONNA ASK HIM TO HATE-MARRY ME.

I DEFEATED ZARDE ONCE, I CAN BRING HIM DOWN AGAIN.
CUTTER! THESE ARE FLEET OPERATIONS, NOT YOUR PERSONAL REVENGE SIMULATOR.
USCS Exemplar

ZARDE MAY BE A BRUTE, BUT I EXPECT ALL OF US TO FUNCTION WITH ALL THE PANACHE AND ZEST ENDEMIC TO THE CREW OF THE PARADIGM.

WHAT HO, BRAVERY! WHAT HO, FRIENDSHIP!
LET'S SHOW THEM THAT THIS IS ONE PARADIGM THAT REFUSES TO SHIFT!

WAS THAT OUR
YES, THAT WAS YOUR PEP TALK.

HOLIDAY, THE PARADIGM NEEDS TO BE A PARAGON OF GENTLEMANLY STRENGTH.
HOW MANY SHOOTERS HAVE WE?
CUBE

CAPTAIN, THIS SHIP HAS 24 MASER BATTERIES AND FOUR CARDINAL-POINT TORPEDO BANKS.
SHE'S GOT ALMOST TWICE THE ARMAMENT OF THE FUSELI.
SPC

SHE'S ALSO PACKING A COVARIANT TYPE VII FORCE SCREEN ARRAY: BACK, FRONT AND DOUBLE-SIDE.
WE'RE CLEARLY GONNA HAVE TO GET YOU UP TO SPEED ON TACTICAL.
CUBE

AGREED. ELSE WE'LL NEVER DEFEAT THE PARADIGM.
... AH, WAIT, THAT'S US. ALL THE BETTER.

THEY'LL TRY TO CORRAL US IN WITH FIGHTER GROUPS, BUT WE HAVE COUNTER-MEASURES.
THE PARADIGM IS BIG ENOUGH TO DEFINE ITS OWN BATTLEFIELD.

PUSHING OUR WEIGHT AROUND! I AM NO STRANGER TO IT.
FRESH OUT OF COLLEGE I STRONG-ARMED MY THESIS INTO BEING PUBLISHED BY CRITICAL THOUGHT QUARTERLY.

MY FATHER'S COLLEGE DEVELOPED THE MAGAZINE'S ENTIRE TECH INFRASTRUCTURE.
IT WAS THAT CONNECTION THAT GOT ME WHAT I WANTED.

I GUESS WHAT I'M ASKING IS, IN A COMBAT SCENARIO, WHO IS THE "MY FATHER?"

TWO HOURS BEFORE MOCK BATTLE
SIR, WE'RE IN TAC GROUP HIBISCUS ALONG WITH THE SUMMER RHYME, THE FALCONER, THREE FIGHTER UNITS AND ONE HEAVY BOMBER WING.
I LIKE IT.

WEAPONS HAVE BEEN REDUCED TO TEST-LEVEL POWER, INCLUDING MOCK TORPEDO LOADOUTS.
SUMPTUOUS!

ENGINEERING! DID YOU PREPARE THE OPENING SALVO I REQUESTED?
YES. YES WE DID.

GOOD LUCK ALL

ATTENTION TAC GROUP HIBISCUS! THIS IS THE EXEMPLAR, YOUR NEW VICTOR.
YOU HAVE ILLEGALLY ENTERED EARTH SPACE. THE PUNISHMENT IS SUPER-DEATH.

I AWAIT YOUR SURRENDER.
EXEMPLAR, THIS IS GROUP LEADER PARADIGM. WE ARE IN RECEIPT OF YOUR REQUEST, BUT -- AUUGH!
SQUEEEEEEEEEEE
CUT THE COM!!

HOW UNSPORTSMAN-LIKE IS THAT?! FLOODING US WITH STATIC!
IT'S CHEAP, BUT YOU HAVE TO ADMIT IT WORKS.

GET THE EXEMPLAR BACK ON, LET'S GIVE HIM A LITTLE OF OUR OWN STATIC!
SQUEEEEEEE EEEE
AUGH!

SHE'S DEPLOYING FIGHTERS! HOW MANY BAYS DOES SHE HAVE?
FOUR. THE EXEMPLAR IS A SUPERCARRIER.

V-BEAM, IT'S JUST LIKE I SAID! ZARDE'S FIGHTERS ARE MOVING TO FLANK US! HE WANTS US TO TURN OUR REAREND TOWARDS HIS BROADSIDE!
CUTTER, TARGET THOSE FINS. GIVE HIM A SPORTING CHANCE.

WE HAVE A STRAIGHT SHOT AT HER MICROFUSION SUBASSEMBLY --
PATIENCE, CUTTER! ZARDE NEEDS TO KNOW THE KIND OF GENTLEMEN HE'S DEALING WITH.

REGISTERING COSMETIC HITS TO OUR MAIN VENTRAL FIN, CAPTAIN.
VENTRAL?!? THAT'S OUR BEST FIN!!

THE EXEMPLAR IS POWERING MASERS! I GUESS YOU RILED UP ZARDE!
HER FIGHTERS WILL BE IN FIRING RANGE IN 20 SECONDS.
SCREEN ARRAYS, MR. JINX!

DASH OFF SOME FLAK WHILE WE'RE AT IT. WHAT RANGE CAN WE GET WITH THAT?
BEAMS! IF YOU DON'T KNOW WHAT YOUR SHIP CAN DO, WE'RE SUNK!
VERMILLION ALERT

SHIPS DON'T SINK IN SPACE, MR. EDGEWISE.
PERHAPS THE KEY TO SUCCESS LIES WITHIN PURE INSTINCT!

TACTICAL -- FIRE A WEAPON OF YOUR CHOOSING AT AN IMPORTANT PART OF SOMETHING.
... MAKE IT TWO IMPORTANT PARTS! WE MEAN BUSINESS.

OUR FIGHTERS ARE SCRAMBLING, SIR. HOSTILE BOMBER GROUP INBOUND.
SO LET'S SEAR THEM WITH OUR SAVOROUS HEAT!

... WAIT, IS THIS RIDICULOUS? IS THIS A RIDICULOUS THOUGHT I JUST HAD?
YES, AND WHAT IS IT?

HOW ACCURATE ARE OUR WEAPONS? COULD WE... PINPOINT THE BOMB THE BOMBER IS CARRYING?
THOSE ESCORTS ARE AWFULLY CLOSE.

THAT'S... GENIUS! THAT'S AS CLOSE AS I'VE EVER BEEN TO WANTING TO GIVE YOU A PIRATE HANDSHAKE.
WHAT'S --
NOPE. THE MOMENT'S OVER.

HITS REGISTERED, SIR! PARADIGM KNOCKED OUT OUR TAC BOMBER WITH A WELL-PLACED MASER.
GET THAT ESCORT REGROUPED!

ESCORT TOOK DAMAGE FROM THE BLAST. THEY'RE PULLING OUT.
WHAT?! BUT THERE WERE NO EXPLOSIONS!!

THIS IS ALL SIMULATION, CAPTAIN. YOU HAVE TO FOLLOW THE BATTLE REPORT.
AUGH! THIS DOESN'T FEEL RIGHT!

SUMMER RHYME IS FIRING ON OUR SECOND BOMBER GROUP.
PYEW! PYOW BWOMMMKSSRRCH AUGH! THIS SUCKS!

MORE FIGHTERS INBOUND, APPROACHING FROM AFT.
FIRE OUR SUBLIGHT ENGINES IN SEQUENCE. MORSE OUT "GOOD SHOW, GENTS."
BEAMS! WE'RE GONNA END UP DEAD LAST!

ALSO -- SPOOL OFF SOME CANNONADE.
I DON'T GET YOU AT ALL! A LITTLE WHILE AGO YOU SHOWED A LITTLE TACTICAL INSIGHT. NOW IT'S LIKE YOU'RE JUST BORED!

IT ISN'T LIKE I'M BORED, I AM INCREDIBLY BORED. ALL THIS ZOOMING AROUND AND SHOOTING PRETEND LASERS.
SIGH JINX, ACTIVATE THE COMBAT AUTOPILOT.

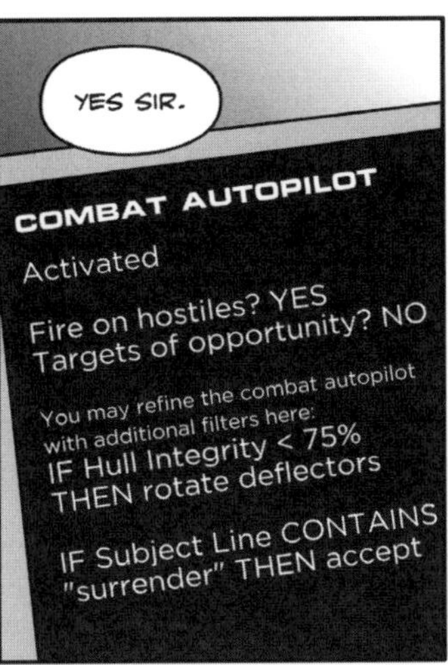
YES SIR.
COMBAT AUTOPILOT
Activated
Fire on hostiles? YES
Targets of opportunity? NO
You may refine the combat autopilot with additional filters here:
IF Hull Integrity < 75% THEN rotate deflectors
IF Subject Line CONTAINS "surrender" THEN accept

WHAT GOOD IS HAVING A TACTICAL OFFICER IF I HAVE TO DEVELOP TACTICS?!
I'M ADVISING YOU! YOU JUST HAVE TO SETTLE ON A PLAN OF ACTION! LIKE A CAPTAIN.

THE ASTRY SHOULD DO THIS VIRTUALLY AND NOT WASTE OUR TIME!
AS I SAY IN MY ESSAY, THE ART OF WAR IN THE AGE OF MECHANICAL SIMULATION.
WELL, I NEVER READ IT!

THAT'S BECAUSE I'M JUST ABOUT READY TO START WRITING IT.
YOU'RE WRITING A THESIS DURING COMBAT?!?

I'M PLAYING TO MY STRENGTHS.
I'M TRYING TO SHOW YOU HOW STUPID YOU ARE, SO DITTO.

WE GOT FIGHTERS SWARMING FROM THE SUMMER RHYME. BUT UNTIL OUR PILOTS GET CLEAR WE CAN'T GET A SOLUTION.
SO WE TAKE DOWN THE RHYME, THEN THE PARADIGM IS DEAD, HOW MANY PILOTS WOULD WE LOSE IF WE JUST OPENED UP ON HER WITH OUR CAPITAL BEAM?

CAPTAIN ZARDE, DID I CATCH YOU IN THE ACT OF OPENING FIRE ON YOUR OWN MEN?!
FOR A GOOD CAUSE! THIS IS WAR!

DO NOT.
SHOOT.
YOUR OWN MEN.
EVEN IF IT IS WITH A SIMULATED MASER!
YES SIR.

TACTICAL... "ACCIDENTALLY" ARM OUR REAL TORPEDOES.
THE SUMMER RHYME IS ABOUT TO HAVE A VERY COLD WINTER.

BUT SIR, WE CAN'T USE A LIVE TORPEDO DURING MOCK COMBAT!
WHY NOT? IT'S OUTSIDE-THE-BOX THINKING!

EVERYONE'S SHIELDS ARE UP FOR SAFETY. A LOW-YIELD TORP WILL STARTLE THE SUMMER RHYME OUT FROM BEHIND THAT CLOUD OF ESCORTS.
THEN WE NAIL HER WITH OUR SIMULATED MASER.

SIR, I WON'T FIRE ON AN ASTRY VESSEL. I RESPECTFULLY DECLINE THAT ORDER.
THEN I'LL DO IT MYSELF, AND YOU'RE RESPECTFULLY DISCHARGED FROM SERVICE!

ARE WE STILL SIMULATING? IS THIS PART OF THE SIMULATION?
I DON'T KNOW, BUT WE'RE TOTALLY SHOOTING A TORPEDO AT THEM.

SIR, MOCK SCREENS ARE AT 35%. WE NEED TO MOUNT AN OFFENSIVE OR THE RHYME WILL FALL.
MR. JINX, THAT IS A TACTICAL OBSERVATION, NOT SCIENCE. YOUR JOB IS JUST STATUS REPORTS.

BIP
SIR, MOCK SCREENS ARE NOW AT 9%.
WAS THAT SO HARD? AND YOU MENTIONED THE RHYME. LOVELY TO SEE THE FUSELI'S SISTER IN ACTIVE SERVICE!

TELEM INDICATES... A LIVE TORPEDO HAS BEEN FIRED BY THE EXEMPLAR!
LIVE?! WHAT THE PIRATE-HELL?! IT'S HEADED STRAIGHT FOR THE RHYME! HER SHIELDS ARE UP, BUT --
????

SUDDENLY I WAS BACK THERE. THAT DAY.
THE LAST DAY I HAD WITH HER.

THE ATTACK ON THE FUSELI.
SABOTEURS RIGGED THE ROYAL SHUTTLE TO EXPLODE, A WARNING TO ANYONE WHO OPPOSED OBDRATH VON LUCIFUGE'S MONOPOLY.
BUT WE SAVED HER AND HER FATHER IN THE NICK OF TIME.

JOVIA! SAY THE WORDS I LONG TO HEAR!
IT WAS SO HOT IN THERE.
CLOSE ENOUGH.

ARE YOU ALL RIGHT, MY PRECIOUS?
I... I'LL BE FINE, MEMNON. DON'T WORRY.
MY FATHER -- !
HE'S HERE AS WELL. HE'S SAFE.

YOU SAVED US. YOU SAVED ME. THE JUPITER COLONIES OWE YOU A DEBT OF GRATITUDE.
I... DID IT FOR MORE SELFISH REASONS THAN THE GOOD OF THE COLONIES.

MEMNON, I --
JOVIA. I'M IN LOVE WITH YOU.

I -- I'M SORRY! I'VE ACTED WITH TERRIBLE IMPULSIVITY! MY BLOOD IS STILL UP FROM MY DARING RESCUE.
IT'S -- I UNDERSTAND. I COMPLETELY DO!

YOU MEAN THAT YOU --
I... THINK I SHOULD REST, MEMNON. WE'LL TALK ABOUT IT THOUGH. WE'LL TALK ABOUT EVERYTHING.
... YES, YES. REST. CONSERVE YOUR LOVELY STRENGTH.

... SOMEONE HAS A GIIIIRLFRIEND!

JOVIA AND HER FATHER WOULD FINISH RECUPERATING AT THE JUPITER COLONIES.
FAREWELL, AMBASSADRIX! I HOPE WE GET THAT CHANCE TO TALK.
WE WILL, MEMNON! I'D LIKE THAT.
AIRLOCK 13

WOW. WHAT WAS THAT LOOK SHE GAVE YOU? I THINK I SHIVERED IN MY TIMBERS A LITTLE BIT.
I WILL NOT ASK FOR CLARIFICATION.

DID SOMETHING HAPPEN BETWEEN YOU AND HER? BEAMS?
PERHAPS, CUTTER, PERHAPS! WE'LL DISCUSS THAT... ANOTHER TIME.

BEAMS? BEAMS! THE ADMIRAL --
HELM, FULL SUBLIGHT. TACTICAL, POWER TO ION CANNONS.

TARGET THE EXEMPLAR'S UNMANNED SECONDARY SYSTEMS. ENGINES, WEAPONS ARRAYS, SCREEN EMITTERS.
VANDERBEAM, THIS IS MADNESS!
I KNOW.

THE EXEMPLAR HAS US OUTGUNNED, AND HER CAPTAIN IS A MADMAN.
THIS INFANTILE TRAINING EXERCISE IS RAPIDLY TURNING INTO AN INFANTILE WAR ZONE.
I CAN'T DO THIS ALONE.

I NEED THE INSIGHT OF A COMPLETELY DERANGED MAN.
A TWITCHY, MONSTROUS INEBRIATE AS VOLATILE AS OUR SICK, VACANT ADVERSARY. A VERITABLE RAPIST OF SENSE.

YOU CAN TAKE YOUR REQUEST FOR INSIGHT AND CRAM IT --
HOW QUICKLY CAN YOU GET STRAIGHT UP CRUNK?
YOU HAVE MY SWORD.

EXTREMELY SHORTLY
OKAY, HERE-SH WHAT WE'RE DOIN'. COME IN HARD ON HER SIX, BUT WE'RE GONNA LIGHT UP HER UNDERBELLY.
WOW, OKAY.

FOCUSH ION CANNONS ON ALL THE POINTY PARTS, THAT'SH HER HEAT SINKS AND WHEN THOSE GO, SHE'LL LOSE POWER FOR LIKE SIX SECONDS.
EXCELLENT! MR. JINX, MAKE SURE WE'VE GOT THAT TARGETING DATA!

AND THEN WE HEAVE TO AND CUTLASS HER FROM TAILFIN TO PROW! ARRR!
CUTTER, NO!

YO HO HO CROW'S NEST AND RUM ON THE PLANK
CUTTER! NEVER GO FULL PIRATE!

WEAPONS FREE! BRING OUR TOPSIDE CLOSE TO THE EXEMPLAR, HELM. I WANT TO SEE HER FINEST HAIRS.
FIRING AT WILL!
VZATK

CAPTAIN! THE PARADIGM IS KNOCKING OUT POWER TO WEAPONS!
SIMULATED OR REAL?!
REAL! THEY'RE FIRING IONS!
WARNING

EXEMPLAR TO PARADIGM, CEASE FIRE!
WE JUST HAD A WEAPONS MALFUNCTION IS ALL! EVERYONE'S FINE! DON'T GET SO TOUCHY!

YOU'RE A BAD CAPTAIN, ZARDE. PEOPLE LIKE YOU ONLY LEARN BY BEING TOUCHED, AND HARD.
AND YOU WILL GREATLY DISAPPROVE OF WHERE THESE MEN PUT THEIR HANDS.
OH MY GOD.

PARADIGM, WHAT THE SPACE ARE YOU DOING?! STAND DOWN!
ADMIRAL! WE ARE NEUTRALIZING THE EXEMPLAR! A LIVE WEAPON WAS FIRED IN THE MIDDLE OF COMBAT EXERCISES!

I'LL DEAL WITH ZARDE! DISOBEY MY ORDERS AND YOU'LL BE DUSTING VASES IN A MUSEUM AGAIN!
SHOWS WHAT YOU KNOW. MR. JINX ALWAYS DID THAT!
YEAH, SIR.

FIRING ON AN ASTRY VESSEL IS AN ACT OF TREASON!
TELL THAT TO ZARDE AND HIS SUPPOSED ACCIDENT!

LOOK, I MESSED UP! CAN'T WE JUST FORGIVE ME AND NAME ME THE WINNER LIKE ALWAYS?

THE FLEET IS CLOSING ON THIS POSITION, SIR.
BEAMS... YOU MADE A STAND. THAT'S WHAT COUNTS.
I AM DISCOVERING THIS, YES.

MULTIPLE READINGS -- TWO DOZEN PLUS WARCRUISERS ARE POWERING IONS.
NO DOUBT TO SEAL OUR TREASONOUS FATE.
HOPEFULLY THEY WILL LEAVE OUR LIFE SUPPORT INTACT, LEST THIS BECOME AN INSTANT, FATAL COURT MARTIAL.

THEY'RE OPENING FIRE.
PREPARE FOR IMPACT!

DIRECT HIT -- TO THE EXEMPLAR. THEY'RE FIRING ON ZARDE, SIR!
PREPARE FOR SMUG SATISFACTION!

THE FLEET IS RALLYING AROUND US! THEY'RE NOT TAKING IT FROM ZARDE ANYMORE!
IT'S A MASSIVELY MULTIPLAYER MUTINY!
ADMIRAL AIN'T BE LIKING THAT.

ASSEMBLED FLEET, STAND DOWN! I SHOULD THROW YOU ALL IN THE BRIG, INCLUDING YOUR SHIPS!
BUT THERE IS NO BRIG LARGE ENOUGH.
IT'S A RIDICULOUS NOTION.

CAPTAIN ZARDE, I'M HEREBY RELIEVING YOU OF DUTY.
WE'LL TALK ABOUT HOW PERMANENT IT MAY BE AFTER YOU'RE ESCORTED TO EARTH.

MEANWHILE, FLEET EXERCISES ARE CANCELLED, ALONG WITH ANY AND ALL SHORE LEAVE FOR THE NEXT SIX MONTHS.
AND ENGINEERING CORPS -- I WANT TO SEE PLANS FOR A SHIP-BRIG ON MY DESK TOMORROW MORNING.

THIS WAS THE WORST FLEET EXERCISE I'VE EVER PARTICIPATED IN, AND THAT INCLUDES ALL THE ONES I DID ON YOUR SHIP.
YOU'VE DONE OTHERS?
NOPE.

AS THE STARCON FLEET DISPERSES, THOUGH, WHO'S TO SAY WE AREN'T TAKING AWAY SOMETHING MORE IMPORTANT?
LIKE SHAME?

THERE'S NO SHAME IN WHAT WE DID.
YOU FELT THIS WAS IMPORTANT, AND YOU WERE RIGHT. I THOUGHT IT WAS RIDICULOUS, AND I WAS RIGHT TOO.
WINNERS ALL.

WELL. I GUESS KNOWING ZARDE RUINED HIS CAREER IS BETTER THAN A DUMB TROPHY.
IT'S AS THOUGH HIS LIFE BECAME OUR TROPHY!
YEAH!

FOR A MOMENT I WAS BACK THERE. WITH JOVIA.
FOR A MOMENT ALL OF THIS SEEMED SO... COLORLESS IN COMPARISON.

BUT HAVE I LOST HER FOR GOOD? THE TIMESUIT IS LONG GONE.
KATARAKIS MADE OFF WITH IT OVER A YEAR AGO AND HASN'T TURNED UP SINCE.

FATE! ENEMY OF DESIRE! WHAT CONFOUNDING TWISTS WILL YOU PRESENT ME WITH?!

TODAY IS YOUR DENTIST APPOINTMENT, SIR.
I'LL... PONDER THIS OMEN.

EPILOGUE.
THIS WAS THE LAST STRIKE.
THERIN ZARDE, YOU ARE DISHONORABLY DISCHARGED FROM THE STARCON ASTRY. DO YOU HAVE ANYTHING TO SAY?
YES. YOU ALL ARE BARF-HEADS.

MEN, SEE THIS HUMAN GARBAGE TO A CELL. WE'LL START THE SENTENCING PROCESS NEXT WEEK.
SPOKEN LIKE A TRUE BARF-HEAD.

ARRGH! I REALLY THOUGHT THAT'D GET HIM STEAMED.
I CAN'T GET ANYTHING RIGHT THESE DAYS!

WHAT IF YOU HAD ANOTHER CHANCE TO GET THINGS RIGHT... ?

EARTH. OFFICE OF THE DIRECTOR.
TECHFAB, YOU ARE MY MOST TRUSTED ENGINEERING ROBOT.
THAT'S SO KIND OF YOU TO SAY, DIRECTOR.

IT'S TRUE.
AS YOU KNOW I'VE BEEN GOING BACK AND FORTH WITH TITANS OF INDUSTRY FOR THE LAST YEAR.
YES, THE PROPOSAL FROM... OBDRATH VON LUCIFUGE. DEPOSED CEO AND EVILSMITH.
OFFICE OF THE DIRECTOR

I AM OPPOSED TO WORKING WITH HIM AGAIN, GIVEN THAT I BELIEVE HE MURDERED MY DAUGHTER.
BUT I'M BEING PRESSURED BY THE ENTIRE STARCON ECONOMY.
HAS THE WORLD FORGOTTEN?

WHAT CAN I HELP YOU WITH, DIRECTOR?
EXPLAIN THIS THING TO ME BECAUSE I DON'T UNDERSTAND A WORD OF IT.

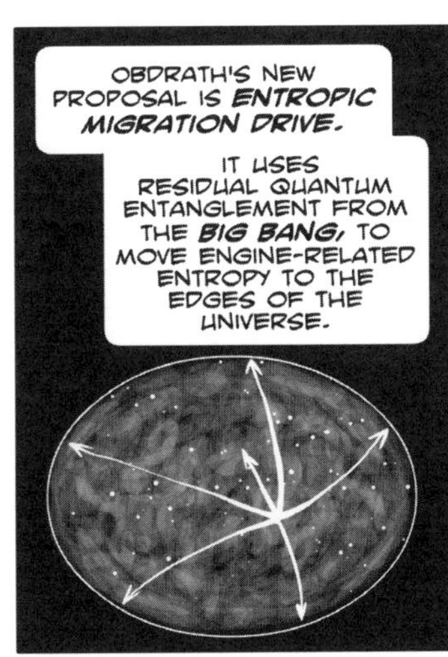
OBDRATH'S NEW PROPOSAL IS ENTROPIC MIGRATION DRIVE.
IT USES RESIDUAL QUANTUM ENTANGLEMENT FROM THE BIG BANG, TO MOVE ENGINE-RELATED ENTROPY TO THE EDGES OF THE UNIVERSE.

DOES HE REALLY BELIEVE THE CONSORTIUM COULD RISE AGAIN?
STARSLIP DRIVE IS SLOW AND EXPENSIVE. EM DRIVE IS FAST AND CHEAP, ALMOST AS FAST AS SHIFT DRIVE.
HE HAS COMMERCE ON HIS SIDE.

OUR... PROPOSALS HAVE FALLEN SO FAR SHORT.

YES, THE IDEAS HAVE BEEN PRETTY DUMB.
INTRODUCING Super STARSLIP
WAY MORE
ARCHES

IF I WORK AGAINST VON LUCIFUGE, IT WILL ONLY SHAKE THE CONFIGURATION'S AILING ECONOMY.
IT MIGHT EVEN CAUSE MEMBER PLANETS TO MOVE AGAINST ME. THE LAST THING THIS GALAXY NEEDS IS VON LUCIFUGE ALONE AT THE HELM AGAIN.
AGREED.

THE ONLY COURSE IS TO SUPPORT ENTROPIC MIGRATION DRIVE, AND KEEP A CLOSE EYE ON HIM FROM THE INSIDE.
AGREED.

... WE'RE AGREED THEN.
SADLY, IN FULL AGREEMENT. THAT SCUMHOUND IS BACK AND IT MAKES MY ORGANS ROIL.

FUN AND COOL
NEW PARTNERSHIP!
VON LUCIFUGE, DIRECTOR JOVOX BOAST NEW HORIZONS, FRIENDSHIPS
IS A NEW ENGINE IN THE WORKS?

UGH. IT'S TAKEN EVERY SCRAP OF VC I COULD PULL TOGETHER TO GET ENTROPIC DRIVE OFF THE GROUND.
EVERY FAVOR CALLED IN, EVERY CORNER CUT, EVERY PENNY SAVED.

AT LONG LAST, I'M WITHIN SHOOTING RANGE OF SOME SEMBLANCE OF MY PREVIOUS SEAT OF POWER.

JOVOX THINKS HE CAN PLACATE ME BY PRETENDING TO SUPPORT MY RETURN...
BUT I KNOW WHAT HE'S UP TO. IT'S ONLY A MATTER OF TIME BEFORE --

GREG! DID YOU LEAVE THE FRIDGE DOOR OPEN?!
OOPS. SORRY, MAN.
THE CARTON?! YOU'RE THE WORST ROOMMATE EVER!

SAW YOUR THING ON THE NEWS, MAN. KINDA COOL.
THAT "PRETTY COOL THING" IS POISED TO BRING BACK THE CONSORTIUM AND EARTH'S DOMINION OVER KNOWN SPACE.
THAT'S SO SICK.

... WHY IS MY HELLFONT DISCHARGER IN THE KITCHENETTE NOOK?
UH.
WHAT IS THIS... WHAT IS THIS, IT LOOKS LIKE BURNED SALAD --
DUDE.

I NEED THIS DISCHARGER TO PURGE HELLISH ENERGY BUILDUP FROM MY FOREBRAIN!
WHATEVER MAN. MAYBE I NEEDED IT TO... PURGE... STRESS BUILDUP FROM MY BRAIN.

I WAS ONCE THE MOST POWERFUL FIGURE IN THE GALAXY.
DO NOT USE MY STUFF AS BONGS.

WHATEVER, BRO. YOU'RE THE ONE WHO WAS LOOKING FOR A ROOMIE.
I'D BE LIVING WITH MY OLD ASSISTANT JEAN IF SHE HADN'T BEEN TRAGICALLY KILLED IN THAT MURDERING CONTEST ON PRAVA III.

I PAY MY HALF OF THE RENT, AND WE DIVVIED UP CHORES. THAT'S ALL I'M ON THE HOOK FOR.
DON'T GET BENT BECAUSE I GOT A DIFFERENT LIFESTYLE THAN YOU, DUDE.

I HOPE YOUR THING TO TAKE OVER THE UNIVERSE OR WHATEVER WORKS OUT. YOU'RE A COOL GUY.
SORRY I GOT UP IN YOUR BUSINESS.
WELL... APOLOGY ACCEPTED.

IT'S YOUR TURN TO DO THE DISHES ANYWAY.
YOU NEVER PRESOAK!

SO WHAT'S HOW THIS THING WORKS YOU'RE MAKIN'?
OH MY GOD. I'LL EXPLAIN IT IF YOU STOP TALKING.

ENTROPY INCREASE, OR THE INCREASE OF DISORDER, IS IMPOSSIBLE TO STOP.
WHEN WE BURN FUEL, THE HIGHER-ENERGY "ORDER" OF THE FUEL MOLECULES IS SPENT TO GET AT THAT ENERGY.

ENTROPY ALWAYS INCREASES, BUT BY EXPLOITING QUANTUM ENTANGLEMENT,
I CAN NOW SHUNT THAT ENTROPY SOMEWHERE FAR AWAY. WE GET ALL THE BENEFITS, BUT NONE OF THE LOSS OF ORDER.

SORT OF LIKE WHEN I HIDE MY DIRTY SOCKS UNDER THE COUCH.
IF THE COUCH WAS BILLIONS OF LIGHT YEARS AWAY.
HOW I WISH THAT WERE TRUE.

I'M NOT GONNA BE AROUND IN THE NEXT COUPLE WEEKS.
COME ON, MAN! WHAT ABOUT MADDEN '44?

I HAVE NO TIME FOR GAMES. NOT EVEN WITH THE APARTMENT 33A CHAMPIONSHIP ON THE LINE.
THE PUBLIC CONSIDERS ME AN EVIL MAN, DUE TO SOME CHOICES THAT I'VE MADE.

CHOICES ANYONE ELSE WOULD HAVE MADE IF THEY WERE THE WEALTHIEST, MOST POWERFUL CEO IN KNOWN SPACE.
SO I'VE HIRED AN IMAGE CONSULTANT.

TIME FOR OBDRATH VON LUCIFUGE TO GET FUNKY FRESH.
THAT... IS LITERALLY 1,600 YEARS OLD.
WORD OUT.

HELLO, MR. VON LUCIFUGE. MY NAME IS XULA AND I'M YOUR STYLE CONSULTANT.
I CAN'T WAIT TO GET TO WORK ON MANUFACTURING MY GOOD NAME!

FORGET ABOUT YOUR PAST -- FIRST THING, WE NEED TO UNDERSTAND HOW YOU'RE PERCEIVED AT FIRST GLANCE.

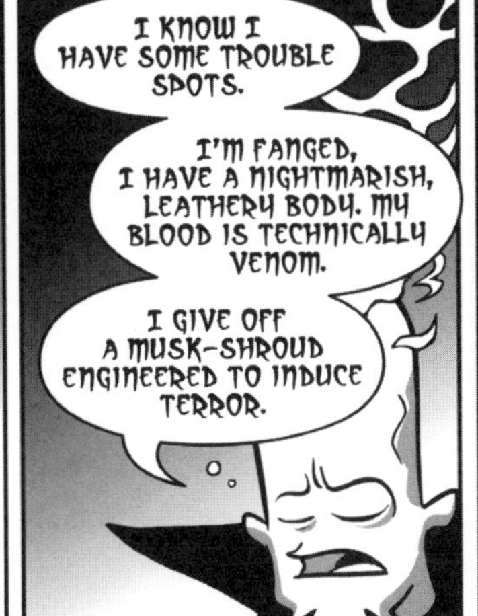
I KNOW I HAVE SOME TROUBLE SPOTS.
I'M FANGED, I HAVE A NIGHTMARISH, LEATHERY BODY. MY BLOOD IS TECHNICALLY VENOM.
I GIVE OFF A MUSK-SHROUD ENGINEERED TO INDUCE TERROR.

CAN WE AT LEAST PLUG THAT FLAMING HOLE UP THERE?
WELL, IT'S SORT OF A TRADEMARK. PLUS I'D DIE.

WE'VE DONE A COUPLE OF MOCKUPS TO SEE WHAT YOU THINK OF YOUR POTENTIAL NEW IMAGE.
WONDERFUL. THE SOONER THIS IS OVER, THE BETTER.

CASUAL
HAPPY!!
NO FACIAL HAIR
HMM... HIDE THE

CLASSY, UNDERSTATED
AGAIN NO BEARD
CLASSY PUFFS WAFTING

WHAT ABOUT THIS?
KISS THE CEO
JUST... JUST BE A GREAT CHEF.

OVER.
BETTER.

BACK SO SOON?
YES. MY IMAGE CONSULTANT TAUGHT ME WHAT IT MEANS TO HAVE AN IMAGE.

YOUR IMAGE IS SOMETHING YOU CULTIVATE YOUR WHOLE LIFE LONG, WITH YOUR ACTIONS.
YOU CAN'T CHANGE IT WHEN THINGS GET TOUGH.

I GUESS WE BOTH HAVE OUR LITTLE IMAGE ISSUES TO DEAL WITH.
MAYBE WE'RE MORE ALIKE THAN I THOUGHT, GREG.

URP.
FFSHHWWP.

Notes on the Reboot and Storyline Discussion

If this is your first time reading, welcome.

Starslip used to be called *Starslip Crisis*, and the first storyline in this collection tries to bridge the two. My goal was to soft-reboot the strip and clean up—or at least shelve—some of the more confusing parts of continuity. Sort of like how Bruce Wayne is technically 90 years old, but you can read in-continuity *Batman* stories today where there aren't a million editor's notes and explanations.

The strip changed its setting from a traveling intergalactic art museum to an armed exploratory cruiser, making it more traditional sci-fi. All the original cast's impulses are the same though, and Vanderbeam is still a glorified curator trying to understand the universe through that tiny lens.

After The Rockets Calm *(page 7)*

The first panel of the first strip matches the last panel of the last strip in *Starslip Crisis: Volume 3*. So we learn that the potential to find the closest parallel universe may end up shifting people in time as well. You can also see me evolving Vanderbeam's look, to a degree. Here everyone is wearing their *Crisis*-era costumes, but I changed how Vanderbeam's head and jaw connected to his neck.

This storyline also wrecks one of the pivotal moments of *Starslip Crisis*, where Vanderbeam tells Jinx to wear the Spine of the Cosmos "like a hat" to recontextualize its meaning and free everyone who was enslaved by it. So in this universe, that famous line never actually gets said by anyone.

Vanderbeam is sometimes a tough character to write, because in the reboot I wanted him to be a little more brash and proactive, and not just a terrible captain. Now he has the potential to be a sort-of-good captain, except he brings the wrong skillset to the table. I tried to show this by letting his knowledge of art and culture give him insight into how Katarakis' World-Ship would have specific weakpoints.

This storyline also removes both Katarakis and Deep Time as threats the big issue with *Crisis*—that I felt necessitated a reboot—was that if Vanderbeam had access to a timesuit, he would have ignored everything else and tried to learn how to use it to take him back to Jovia. If there was something else going on, he would have been distracted by the promise of that suit technology.

So making Katarakis abscond with it sets him up as a villain for later, and lets Vanderbeam throw himself fully into being a captain. He no longer has possession of the answer. It's out there, somewhere.

Paradigm Shift *(page 14)*

I chose the name *Paradigm* for the new ship so I could do that title for the storyline. I like the word and I like that it has a weird spelling. Here were the runners-up, with my notes:

> *Hyperion*. A sturdy ship name, but it's also the name of the treatment plant where my dad occasionally worked. So it would have been an in-joke. (He was a wastewater engineer before he retired, and his love of physics and science is a big part of why *Starslip* exists.)
>
> *Paragon*. A great word but I've heard it used too much.
>
> *Patriarch*. A Vanderbeamy word. I was very close to using this one.
>
> *Crimson Fall*. I considered christening the new ship the *Crimson Fall*, the *Fuseli's* old handle, but decided it would get too confusing.
>
> *Archhammer*. I liked this one until I realized I was just remembering the name of the Star Destroyer from the *Star Wars* game *Dark Forces*: the *Arc Hammer*. Oops.
>
> *Arc Matron*. Still hadn't given up on the parental thing, or the Arc thing.
>
> *Ferrix*. I don't know, I just like Xs.
>
> *Shieldsword*. This was an anime-style weapon I came up with for a project that

went nowhere. I just wrote the word to see if it looked good.

Sybaris. A city notorious for its luxury.

Falconer. I thought of this because of its mention in the Yeats poem *The Second Coming*, which figured heavily into the entire plot of *Crisis*.

Exemplar. A cool word, and a little bombastic, so perfect for a big ship. I recycled it for Zarde's ship name.

"Paradigm Shift" also introduces the Ten Protocols, which in the confines of the strip are never actually laid out. The reboot was patterned after the Star Trek triptych of a Brash Captain, a Cold Scientist and a Emotional Doctor. I wanted to replace the lattermost with an Emotional Lawyer, as if in the future it was more important to have your legal ducks in a row than to ensure the health of the crew. The Lawyer, Quine, is bound by not one but ten vague prime directives that sound great but can't possibly be followed.

In this story Holiday offhand-mentions that she worked aboard a far-core station, which we get to see one of in a later storyline not in this collection. I always wanted to flesh Holiday out and make her more real. This is another example of my love for *Star Trek: Deep Space Nine*—hopefully I will get a chance to show Holiday interacting with the old crew of that station in a flashback.

Starslip gets a new doctor character with Dahk Tohrr, a shape-changing Moliff. The character idea was all Scott Kurtz. Dahk is not an incompetent doctor, like Futurama's Dr. Zoidberg. Dahk is very good, just not at shape-changing. I have seen very, very little Futurama and have tried to stay ignorant of it for fear of subconsciously copying elements of it.

The new relevator further displays the United Star Configuration's apathy about other cultures and places; it just destroys whatever is beneath it with as much noise and fanfare as possible.

Worst Contact *(page 25)*

I really, really enjoyed this storyline. I adapted it from the first script for a *Starslip* comic book (that I talk about at length in Volume 3). Quine was such an interesting character and an interesting line to walk—he couldn't be as spineless as Jinx, but he needed to be ineffectual. Plus, how interesting Jovia's death was handled the way it was, only to introduce a character that constantly dies with no sadness felt whatsoever!

The Quel were fun to play with. Science fiction gets away with too, too many stories where the "aliens" are just humans with extra strength or extra powers, but all their motivations and lives are interchangeable. I really wanted to write alien races that we would be baffled by. The Quel are powerful, advanced, and peaceful, and their total hive mind has given them a comfort that supercedes their curiosity about the universe. Humans all want, want, want. What kind of aliens could just be satisfied with their situation indefinitely?

In the original story, the captain of the ship—then named Trask—was the Kirk-like, swaggering chauvinist who slept with the Quel woman and ruined their hive mind. But the characters were different now and I had to change it, and decided to make it Quine. (It could have easily been Cutter, but I think even he would have been more respectful than that.)

Taken Holiday *(page 40)*

A friend recommended either this very plot, or one very close to it, and it was a perfect way to ground Holiday in something.

In general we've dealt with the old shift drive as a unique means of FTL travel, but it required the knowledge (read: apathy) that you may be screwing over a parallel universe version of your self and your ship in the process. This has always been taken as a risk, and shift drive was supposed to have the infinite number of parallel universes on its side, but over time those odds degraded.

Holiday is a very 30-Rock-Liz-Lemon type of character in that she's fully absorbed by her work, and has no time for real friendships or family. Here she's confronted by the fact that there was at least one universe where she did have it all—a career, a new husband, and even a child on the way.

Anyway, the last thing I want to do is overexplain it. I just wanted the opportunity to flesh out Holiday beyond having an ill-advised secret crush on Vanderbeam.

Anthelerix Polygmeon *(page 45)*

Here's a story I was waiting to tell for a long time. As much as I like television and movie sci-fi, I feel like it generally anthropomorphizes or humanizes all the aliens we encounter. I get it—there's a finite amount of time to get everyone up to speed, so we can't have everyone speaking different languages, breathing different atmospheres, and having radically different customs. Otherwise you'd never get to the laser fight.

But inasmuch as I explored an alien race that was totally satisfied with not exploring anything (the Quel), I also wanted to do a Q-like super-species of godlike entities that had zero interest in mankind whatsoever. In *TNG*, the Q Continuum is obsessed with human morality and decision-making. *Really?* Would they not have fully mined that billions upon billions of years ago?

We like to feel that we are complex, important, and more to the point, in the right when we decide to do the things we do. So here are the Anthelerix, who treat the crew of the *Paradigm* as inquisitive microbes.

They were a lot of fun to design too, and I remember trying to come up with a design that didn't just look like an organic version of the character Vore—I have a soft spot for a tall cylindrical head. The Anthelerix have faces like axes or sharp pendulums.

I envisioned them like great librarians who were content to keep and retain. Maybe their interest would turn to humans someday, but honestly they've probably encountered countless races very similar to humans and have had their fill.

A side note about the Anthelerix: their name is a nonsense phrase from my first webcomic, *Checkerboard Nightmare*. In the strip they're mentioned, Chex asks his robot Vaporware, if he's still around in the future, to find a way to beam a glimpse of the future back to the present. Chex expects ray guns and flying cars, and Vaporware ends up with a glimpse of some inconceivable hybrid alien mass that mention "anthelerix polygmeon," the idea being that Vaporware has somehow merged with them.

As you may know, Vore is just Vaporware driven mad by a thousand years alone in space. So maybe they will link up after all.

Revisiting the *Fuseli (page 56)*

It was time to up the ante a little bit as far as the impossible romance between Princess Jovia and Vanderbeam.

In the *Crisis* era, before the reboot, Jovia really was only a Beatrice-like construct to Vanderbeam's Dante. All we knew was that Jovia might have been okay with Vanderbeam as a person, and was at least grateful to him for the rescue of her and her father, the King of the Jupiter Colonies. Other than that there was no romance. The saddest part of Vanderbeam's struggle with her death wasn't even that he'd lost someone he loved, but someone he might have loved, who might have loved him back. She became a symbol, a glyph for unrequited, unmatured love.

So before the reboot, I think we see Vanderbeam much more driven by this image of Jovia than he actually is driven by a real person. Regrettably I came to look at this as bad writing, and an application of "women-in-refrigerators syndrome," coined by Gail Simone to mean that a lot of women, at their best in comics, die as plot devices to be pined over by the hero to motivate them (I'm paraphrasing). And it is true, I had barely understood who Jovia was before I killed her.

In my mind Jovia honestly did not have a lot to her—she certainly didn't deserve to be assassinated, nor did she do poorly with her efforts to increase awareness of art with the help of the *Fuseli* and its gala fundraisers. She just wasn't a person who had come into her own yet.

At any rate—Vanderbeam deserved to have a little more time saying goodbye to his old ship and his old life, and it was a good opportunity to begin building a real relationship between him and Jovia. It comes back later in this collection, and will at least a few times more before the series ends.

The Moliff-Sarican Dispute *(page 59)*

This storyline took aim at two things: the movie *District 9* (which I enjoyed very much) and the dry backstory of the *Star Wars* prequels (which I did not).

So we open on the senior staff receiving a new mission, to settle some arguments between the agrarian-but-displaced Saricans, and the bizarre alien Moliffs. The dispute was just a way to have fun with the cast using tools that they already had, and to get to know the Moliff species a little better.

There is one exciting reveal for Dahk and his kind that I haven't gotten to in this collection! It's just a sci-fi twist I have been waiting to deploy, but it's interesting. Next book, I promise!

Starslip Mine *(page 67)*

Hopefully the inspiration for this is obvious: the *TNG* episode "Starship Mine" in which Picard is called upon to thwart a group of terrorists that take over an evacuated *Enterprise*. The thrust is similar here, except the hero is Quine, not our captain. We hadn't yet seen the dynamics of Quine's cloning abilities and it was time to put them to the test.

The only part I don't like about this story is how I had to be vague about how Quine's intelligence is transmitted from his body upon death, instantly back to the ship. It had to use some technique that was much more advanced and reliable than the communique system, something that any terrorist would know to jam or disable first.

This storyline is also one of very few examples where I changed the plot based on what readers were predicting. It does happen! At first, the enemy reveal was going to be fan-favorite character Zillion, who I personally can't stand. The giveaway was one of the terrorists saying they couldn't understand a word he was saying. That was too much of a giveaway, and many people guessed that Zillion would return.

However I wasn't sure if that's the way I wanted him to come back, especially since we already have a new space rogue in this story: Crice Ramden. So I came up with a reason to bring back the pirate Infra-Redbeard, who we actually haven't seen since the very beginning of *Starslip Crisis*, four or five years ago. The reason why no one could understand him was his perma-drunk condition which caused his body to occasionally manufacture alcohol in his own bloodstream. Take that, readers! I think Infra-Redbeard was a more fun choice for this storyline anyhow.

How the Jinxlets Saved the Space Zoo *(page 80)*

This story was a cash grab, I'm sorry to say it. Actually there's not a lot to tell about it, other than I wanted to tie up a loose end from the reboot: if the entire universe was destroyed, starting with Jupiter, then what became of the Jinxlets in orbit of Jupiter, in the zoo? There was no rescue attempt. So they all would have died except for Vanderbeam's lone Jinxlet, Hieronymus B'Gosh. Unacceptable.

This seemed like a good way to reintroduce two long-lost characters, The Chronomantic (time-traveling wooer of historical women) and his main squeeze, non-artist Xxxyyy, whom the former spirited away to protect her from the clutches of Deep Time. (It got pretty dense, thus the reboot.)

A lot of people assumed these characters wouldn't come back in any form, but the coolest twist was a suggestion from someone: let the Chronomantic be Vanderbeam's son, but don't say who the mother is. We still don't know if this aged Vanderbeam ends up with Jovia, or just someone else. However we do know that the Chronomantic takes a more active role in chasing women through time, like his father. It was a neat reveal and a callback to something the Chronomantic said to Vanderbeam before the reboot: that they were a lot alike.

Contrary to... well, I don't know if it is popular belief, but this was not planned from the beginning at all. It just lined up adequately.

Finally we end the coloring book story with a scene that shows why we're seeing it presented this way: it's some kind of indoctrination for the most prominent Deep Time agent, Maverick Blazer, who I don't think shows up again for quite a while. After all, Deep Time left once the old shift drive was discontinued and Katarakis was extradited. Surely that's the end of them, right? Right??

Cutter Edgewise, P.I. *(page 87)*

One of my big complaints about science fiction in general is that there's not much of a way to do a traditional detective story. These are worlds in which everything is always logged and recorded at all times. Everything knows where everyone and everything else was, and when, down to the centimeter and the second. Why would there ever be cause for detective work ever again? You could just run the scenario through a simulator and see exactly what happened.

Hard sci-fi would have a lot of problems with this story, but *Starslip* is not hard sci-fi. It's more like sci-fi over-medium. So taking away the ship's logs and making it seem like there were no witnesses was step one. I had been wanting to do a story where Cutter and Jinx team up for some task.

Readers of my work in general will also recognize (at least lookalikes of) Ash and Wade, the two main characters from my short-lived webcomic *F Chords*. I was feeling bad for them and wanted to get them in somewhere so I wouldn't forget about them completely. Disappointingly I had to create a sect of the Quel that wasn't satisfied, which I guess is a natural thing to have happen—it's not like everyone would be happy with not exploring the universe forever. So who would be curious? The ones who didn't have the same access to the hive mind as the others.

Like I mentioned, it's hard to do a detective story in the far future, and I sort of lampshaded that at the very end when they're asking the sunderer how he managed to get past the physical exams and the DNA-accessed rooms. There's too many variables. You plug all those in and all the fun is drained out.

Fleet Exercises *(page 96)*

Like a lot of storylines I do, this one ended up a lot longer and a lot more important than I intended. I write the stories day to day, and although I have an idea of about where it needs to be by the end of the week, I don't really know how I'll get there until the day before.

So here we have the Starcon fleet, in relative disarray, captains still having to learn the limitations of the new starslip drive. I suppose the fleet has done mock battles in the past, but we've never witnessed them in the strip—it stands to reason that despite being the flagship of the Consortium, the *Fuseli* never came out on top.

We also have the return of Therin Zarde, who was Cutter's rival at Blightmoon Academy back in the other universe when Cutter had the captain's chair. Both Zarde and Katarakis, I drew with crazy eyes which is just shorthand for someone who's unbalanced, but at the time my symbol set was so limited that I never meant to imply that Katarakis and Zarde had anything to do with one another. As with the Chronomantic/older Vanderbeam plot point, their connection will be made clearer in the future. It's a good one.

The ships were a lot of fun to draw, and I think the story might have even originated to showcase some more space battles; it seemed like *Starslip* had moved away from them in favor of more *Star Trek*-like planet-surface explorations.

The problem came in when I had this fleet battle going on, but no real... element to tie it together. Usually I know what I want to prove or show or who I want to develop, but here the excuse was just to show a fight in space, without advancing a plot having to do with interstellar war. We hadn't really even met any races worth going to war with. A mock exercise is fun and all, but then what? Vanderbeam loses again? How would he win? He had no taste for it, there was nothing on the line. It was just a game. The only one with any skin in the game was Cutter, and he didn't get to call the shots anymore.

Once I decided the *Fuseli* would have an active sister ship, the *Summer Rhyme*, it started to fall into place. Zarde would go for a truly unorthodox and dangerous tactic, and it would rattle Vanderbeam into a captain's frame of mind once more. I hadn't intended to take us all the way back to the aftermath of Jovia's near-assassination, but it seemed like the right time. There was that love letter left dangling in Vanderbeam's old office. And honestly as we move along some of the details get lost and confused to me. For example—is our Vanderbeam aware of the kiss that took place? I don't think so. We know from the first storyline in this book that Vanderbeam and crew appeared in this version of their universe about four months too late to have rescued Jovia, so our Vanderbeam never experienced that.

It didn't matter. Seeing the *Summer Rhyme* get nailed in the same place that the *Fuseli* took damage in the assassination attempt got Vanderbeam going, and we had our resolution.

Obdrath and Greg *(page 107)*

It had been a while since we saw the old heavies from *Crisis*, and even though it was revealed that Obdrath had been more or less legally exonerated, he hadn't been in a good way since the loss of shift drive. I wanted to bring him back in and show that he was still crawling his way back into running the business. Migrating entropy is something that interested me for a long time, since that's basically what we do when we clean up an oil spill—we trade concentrated mess one place for a worse overall mess over a much larger area. (A metaphor for the human condition?!)

About the Cartoonist

A newly-minted Seattle-ite, Kris Straub is the cartoonist behind the webcomic *Chainsawsuit* and the sci-fi humor saga *Starslip*.

Along with Scott Kurtz he does *Blamimations* for *Penny Arcade TV*. He's also co-author of the Harvey Award-nominated *How To Make Webcomics* published by Image.

Read the further adventures of the crew of the *Paradigm* each week at www.starslip.com, and follow Kris at www.krisstraub.com.